A Tie to the Past

D0815397

A Tie to the Past

David Wiseman

Houghton Mifflin Company
Boston 1989

Library of Congress Cataloging-in-Publication Data

Wiseman, David.
  A tie to the past / David Wiseman. — 1st American ed.
  p. cm.
  Summary: An impulsive prank leaves an English schoolgirl in possession of a box
of personal effects belonging to a now-dead suffragette, whose diary fills her mind and
her dreams with vivid scenes of the struggle for women's voting rights in England in
1909.
  ISBN 0-395-51135-6
  [1. Women—Suffrage—Great Britain—Fiction. 2. England—
Fiction.] I. Title.
  PZ7.W78024Mr   1989   89-7547
  [Fic]—dc19   CIP
                             AC

Printed in the United States of America

P   10   9   8   7   6   5   4   3   2   1

For Katheryn
and in memory of
her great-great-grandmother
who was one of those women
entitled to wear
The Holloway Brooch

A Tie to the Past

Chapter One

Mary Thomson threw the letter down in disgust.

"What is it, Mary?" Miss Taylor asked. "Do you find something to object to?"

"It's always the same," Mary said. "Nobody ever asks what *we* think."

There was a murmur of support from the rest of the class.

"Well, *I'm* asking what you think," the teacher said.

"But it won't make any difference, will it?" Mary objected. "We'll still have to wear the awful stuff."

As Miss Taylor laughed, Mary thought, *even she treats us as if we were half-witted.* "If it matters so much you could try putting your point of view to the Head," the teacher went on. "And there are other changes apart from the new uniform. The school governors are planning to change the name of the school, make it more personal."

"How can they do that?" asked Julia Miller, Mary's friend.

"They're going to call it the Thomas Wilton School."

"Who's Thomas Wilton?" Mary said. "I've never heard of him."

"Well, you will from now on," the teacher announced. "When the name's changed."

"Who is he?" asked Julia.

"Was. He's dead long since. I understand he was a pupil at the school who later became a Member of Parliament. They wanted to give the name of some past pupil to the school, and there didn't seem to be anyone else they could think of."

"And why a man?" said Mary. "Weren't there any women worth remembering?"

The boys in the class groaned. Joe Simpson called out, "Don't listen to her, miss. She's always going on like that, talking about women."

Miss Taylor frowned. "Do you feel seriously about this, Mary?"

Mary glared at Joe Simpson. "I don't see why women should be ignored. They've done as much as men."

"Name one," challenged Joe. "Any girl from the school who's ever done anything to remember her by."

"Well?" said Miss Taylor, looking at Mary.

Mary was silent. She didn't know, but there must be someone. She felt angry and humiliated that she couldn't answer Joe's challenge.

Miss Taylor looked down at her. "If you can think of anyone who's worthy of giving her name to the school, let me know. Perhaps we could persuade the governors to change their minds."

"And what about the uniform, miss?" Julia reminded

her. "Will they change their minds about that? What should we do about it? It's ghastly."

"Ask to see the Head, tell him what you think." She dismissed the class.

"It won't make a bit of difference, going to see old Waddle." Julia said.

"We can try," Mary argued, and, with three of their friends, they marched along the corridor, out of the new building, across to the old part of the school where Mr. Wardle, the Headmaster, had his office.

It made no difference. Mr. Wardle would not even see them. Miss Robinson said, with a grim smile, "He's got too much to do to bother about your objections. The uniform is a perfectly sensible one. I know your parents will think so. So you'd better make sure you give them our letter explaining it. You've all got your letters?"

Mary looked guilty. In her annoyance at the new uniform she had torn her letter up and thrown it away. There was no point in doing that. So, when Miss Robinson dismissed them, she went back to Miss Taylor's classroom and searched in the wastepaper basket to find it.

"Is this what you were looking for, Mary?" Miss Taylor stood at the door holding out a crumpled sheet of paper. She seemed amused. Mary snatched the letter from her, then felt sorry. Miss Taylor was a teacher she liked and respected; she, at any rate, was willing to listen.

"I don't think it's fair, miss."

"So you said."

"I won't wear it."

Miss Taylor nodded as if she understood, then said, "You will, you know. You won't want to be different."

But I am different, Mary said to herself as she left the school to walk home. Julia was waiting for her at the school gate with three other girls.

"I'm not going to wear the new uniform," Julia said.

"Right," said Mary. "Let's agree, now. None of us will wear it, whatever happens. Who on earth could think up such a dull affair — brown, brown, and more brown." She looked at her friends. "Do we agree?" They nodded. "Then we'll all tell our parents. If they object at the parents' meeting, old Waddle is bound to listen."

The others moved away, and Julia and Mary walked slowly along to the main road, where Julia waited to be picked up by her mother. Mary stayed with her until a large silver-gray car, Julia's mother at the wheel, pulled out of the stream of traffic toward them. Mary did not like Julia's mother and knew that Mrs. Miller did not like her, though she pretended she did. Mary wondered if that was because she lived on a council estate while Julia's parents had a large detached house on the edge of town.

That did not seem to matter to Julia. She was good fun, though usually in trouble at school and often in trouble away from it, too. Mary did not always approve of the things Julia did: she cheeked the teachers in a way that made even the nicest of them angry and made Mary uncomfortable; she broke all the school rules, forged absence notes for herself when she wanted a day off, always managed to escape games and was late with her homework, or

4

hurriedly copied it from Mary's in the toilets. And she smoked. She always had plenty of money, but she took her cigarettes from her mother's supply and, according to her, her mother wasn't bothered. Mary knew what would happen to *her* if she was caught smoking.

In spite of all that, Mary was fond of Julia, and she knew Julia liked her. She had overheard Miss Taylor saying, "Those two are as thick as thieves," and she supposed it was true. They had promised to be friends through thick and thin, and, whatever happened, she would never let Julia down. She wondered what Julia and the others would do about the uniform. She expected they would have to give way in the end, but she was determined to make some sort of protest against it.

She handed the school letter to her mother. "It's about a new uniform," she said. "We're not going to wear it, none of us." Her mother glanced at the letter and said, "It sounds very sensible."

"It's horrid," Mary said. "We won't wear it. We're all agreed."

Her mother frowned. "I don't want you getting into any trouble."

"I shan't wear it."

"We'll see about that," her mother said and turned away as if that settled the affair.

"I shan't wear it," Mary said under her breath.

Mary wondered if any of the parents would complain about the new uniform at the parents' evening. Surely they couldn't all think it "sensible," whatever that meant. But when her mother and father came home from the meeting they said nothing about the uniform, though they had plenty to say about Julia Miller.

"Your teachers think she's leading you into bad ways. They wish you could find some other friend."

"There's nothing wrong with her," Mary answered angrily. "And I've plenty of friends. It's just that she's my *best* friend."

"They say you're a sensible girl and would do very well if you could break away from her," her father explained. "We don't want to interfere, we just want you to get on."

She was beginning to hate that word *sensible* and she would not let them separate her from Julia. There was nothing wrong with her friend even if she *was* a bit wild sometimes. And they had agreed to stick together through the uniform protest, whatever happened.

The new uniform was to be introduced with the summer term. Mary did not see Julia during the holidays, so they had no chance to plan a campaign. She wore the uniform on the first day of the term, her mother made sure of that. But she added a few forbidden touches in defiance — a pair of earrings, a bracelet, and a bright yellow and blue neckerchief. Several other girls had done something similar, breaking the rules against jewelry and personal adornment that Miss Robinson, the Deputy Head, was so firm on.

Julia had gone further. She wore the brown skirt and blouse and tie, but she had a pair of crimson stockings, fashionably patterned, and a pair of high-heeled custom-made shoes of the same startling color.

Miss Robinson, eagle-eyed as usual, spotted her immediately. She stared at Julia, opening and closing her mouth as if gasping for breath; then, as Julia smiled sweetly at her, she reddened angrily and snapped, "My room, miss!" Julia, with a careless toss of the head, went to Miss Robinson's room.

"I'm going too," Mary announced loudly and followed her friend, with seven other girls trooping after them. They stood outside the room, uneasily aware of their foolhardiness, waiting for the wrath of authority to descend on them.

"Now for it," Julia said defiantly as the footsteps of the Headmaster and Miss Robinson echoed along the corridor, purposeful and threatening. Joe Simpson and another boy passed, shook their heads in mock disapproval, whispered something to each other, snickered, and went on. Mary was furious.

"Well," blustered Mr. Wardle. "What's this, a mutiny?"

"A deputation," said Mary without thinking.

"Nothing of the kind," said Miss Robinson.

"I'm not in the habit of receiving deputations," said Mr. Wardle. "I'll deal with you one at a time."

"And take off all those ridiculous ornaments," Miss Robinson said. "You know it's against school rules." She looked hard at Mary and then at Julia. "We'll deal with you first, Miss Miller."

"We're all in this together," Mary announced, standing beside Julia, but she heard a gasp from the girls behind her.

"Well?" Miss Robinson said, challenging the other girls.

"I'm sorry, Miss Robinson," Janet James said and removed her bangles. The other girls meekly took off their bits of jewelry and waited for Miss Robinson's approval. "Off you go, then," she said with a self-satisfied smile. "And don't let me see you got up like that again." The girls scuttled off, leaving Mary and Julia to face the anger of Miss Robinson and the Headmaster on their own.

"Now, miss," said Miss Robinson. "In you go." Julia went into the room, but when Mary tried to follow her she found the door closed in her face. She stood, a little afraid now that she was on her own, wondering how she had found the courage to stand up to Miss Robinson. She had never done this sort of thing before. But she and Julia were in this together. They had every right to object to having to wear a uniform that made them look like the inmates of some prison! She tried to hear what was being said on the other side of the door but could make no sense of the jumble of voices. Once she imagined a cry of protest from Julia, then silence fell. At last the door opened and Julia emerged, face flushed and eyes red as if she had been crying. She fled past Mary and Mary turned to follow her. "Mary!" she heard Miss Robinson call, and then again, "Mary! Come back here! At once!" But she could not go back. Julia needed her.

Her friend rushed along the corridor and out of school. There she stopped to let Mary catch up with her. "I hate them," she said.

Mary had never seen her so angry or upset. "What is it?"

"They've suspended me. Told me I should know better

than to behave like that, coming from the sort of family I do. What's that got to do with it?''

"Suspended?''

"Until I apologize for what I said.'' She walked away from the school and, without hesitation, Mary followed. If Julia was suspended she would not go to school either. They had no right to treat her friend like that.

"What *did* you say?''

"I called Miss Robinson a frowsty old frump.'' She laughed. "You should have seen her face. It went so red I thought she was going to burst.'' She laughed again, then turned to look back at the school. Everything was quiet, everyone busy at work. For a moment Mary was sorry she was outside. Apart from the occasional stupid rules she enjoyed school, and this term was important. In twelve months' time exams would be on them, and she meant to do well.

"What are you going to do?'' Julia asked. "There's no need for you to get into trouble as well.''

"We'll stick together,'' Mary answered, but she had a moment's doubt until Julia put her arm through hers and held it tightly.

"We'll stick together,'' Julia echoed.

"How was the first day of term?'' Mary's mother asked.

"So-so,'' said Mary. She hated lying, but she couldn't tell her mother she had spent her day wandering the streets.

"Haven't you any homework?'' Her mother was surprised that she hadn't settled down to work as she usually did.

9

"Not yet," she said. She wondered when her mother would find out what had happened. She was sure the school would get in touch with home if she didn't go back quickly.

"What's wrong?"

"Nothing, Mum, honestly," she answered. But she wasn't being honest. Something *was* wrong. She didn't want to let Julia down, but she didn't want to miss school or get into further trouble. She tried to put it out of her mind, settling down to read one of the novels on the reading list, but she couldn't rouse any interest in a book when her own problems were so difficult.

It was no easier when morning came. She put on her uniform, without adding any defiant touches, and set off from home at the usual time; but she went, as they had arranged, to meet Julia in a snack bar in town.

They sat drinking coffee until after the time for the start of school. Mary couldn't help wishing she were back there, especially as she would be missing one of her favorite lessons — history — and one of her favorite teachers, Miss Taylor. She would go back tomorrow; she had shown Julia she supported her, and that was enough. She was about to tell Julia of her decision when her friend got up from the table and left the snack bar. Mary followed.

"I know what I'm going to do," Julia said. "I'll show them."

"I don't understand."

"They said they were surprised that anyone from a family like mine behaved the way I did. Why should I always be expected to behave myself? What's my family got to do with it?"

"I still don't know what you're getting at."

10

"Let's do something, something dangerous."

"Like what?"

"I'll think of something. Just something to show them I'm not what they expect. I'm different." She walked off. Mary hesitated, then followed. She had seen Julia in this mood before. It usually led to trouble.

They walked away from the snack bar until they came to a small park, a haven of green grass and colorful flower beds, set in a square of tall and dignified houses. Most of the benches in the park were occupied by elderly men and women enjoying the morning sun, but there was an empty bench in the shade of a spreading linden tree. They sat there and Julia took out a packet of cigarettes and offered it to Mary.

"No, thanks," said Mary. Julia shrugged and lit a cigarette for herself. A woman passing by turned to look at her with marked disapproval.

"Nosy old cow!" Julia said under her breath, but Mary thought the woman looked pleasant, a bit like her grandmother, only perhaps a little older. She carried a shopping basket and went across the park toward the main street.

"I know her," said Julia. "At least I know of her, Mrs. Watkins. She's made of money. She lives over there." She gestured toward the Georgian houses on the other side of the park. She threw her unfinished cigarette on the ground and put her foot on it. "I'll teach her to turn her nose up at me. Come on."

"Where?"

"Her house. We'll see what's in it. All these treasures of hers. Come on," she added impatiently as Mary hung back.

11

"We can't."

"*I* can," said Julia. "You can do what you like. Stay outside and keep watch."

"No," Mary said. "You shouldn't."

Julia looked scornfully at her. "You're scared."

"It's wrong."

"Well, I'm going in. I want to see what there is, whether it's true she's got a fortune hidden there. Coming?"

"No," said Mary.

"Then keep watch." And before Mary could protest any further, Julia was walking round to the back of the house looking for a way in. Mary followed, anxious to stop Julia from doing anything silly. But Julia was determined. She opened a gate into the back garden of the house and walked between the straggling weeds up the path to the back door. It yielded at her touch, and Julia stealthily went inside. Mary wanted to call her back but didn't dare to raise her voice. She thought they might be observed from the neighboring houses, but the walls between the gardens were high and large old trees overhung the area and shaded her from view. She looked nervously about her. She should have stopped Julia. Perhaps she should go into the house herself and argue with her. But she had been told to keep watch and she supposed now that Julia was inside that was the best thing to do.

She caught a glimpse of Julia through the back window, opening the drawers of a large kitchen cabinet and impatiently closing them. Then she moved out of sight, going somewhere else in the house. It was so quiet that Mary could hear her friend's footsteps.

But they weren't Julia's footsteps; they were slower,

12

more hesitant, coming from the passage at the back of the houses and approaching the garden gate. Mary waited a moment until she could be sure and then, as the gate began to open, she rushed into the house to warn Julia. She called, softly at first, "Julia, Julia." Then, as no answer came, she called a little more loudly, "Julia! Quick! She's coming!" She felt something rub against her legs and looked down to see a large ginger cat. She leaned down to stroke it and then, realizing the danger they were in, she called again.

"Oh hell!" she heard Julia say. "I'm coming." Julia appeared from the front of the house, carrying something under her arm. She ran to the front door, but when she couldn't open it, she dashed back to Mary. They stood, uncertain for a moment, and then, as the steps slowly approached up the garden path, Julia dashed through the kitchen to the back door and out into the garden, still carrying her burden, and pushed past an old lady who was just reaching to open the door. The woman, astonished, slipped and fell as Julia knocked into her. Mary stopped a moment, wanting to help her up, but Julia called, "Come on. She's all right." Mary ran after Julia but turned at the gate to reassure herself that the old lady was not hurt. She was struggling to her feet, surrounded by her groceries.

"Come on," Julia said crossly. "You'll be caught."

They ran along the alley and turned a corner and then Julia stopped. "You go that way and I'll go this. We don't want to be seen together. Here. Take this." She thrust what she had been carrying into Mary's arms and walked off, looking unconcerned, as if out for a quiet stroll.

Mary glared after her, angry at the way Julia had left her,

13

making her responsible for whatever it was she had taken. What could she do with it? She didn't want it. She should take it back and half-turned to do so when she heard footsteps hurrying along the passage; she panicked and ran, twisting and turning round corners into strange streets until she thought she was safe.

But she wasn't safe, couldn't be while she had stolen goods in her hands. For that was what they were, stolen goods. Julia had burgled the house and she was an accomplice; there was no escaping that. She remembered what Miss Taylor had said, "Those two are as thick as thieves." That was exactly right. They were. Thieves.

Chapter Two

Mary looked at the package. It was wrapped in brown paper and was heavy. Mary had no idea whether it was rubbish or something of value. Whatever it was she wished she hadn't ever handled it. She thought of leaving it somewhere by the roadside where it might be found and returned to Mrs. Watkins. But that way it might never get back to her. She should take it back to the old lady herself, but she didn't dare.

She was cross with Julia, more than ever before, and called to mind all the things her parents had said. "She's a bad influence." "She will lead you astray." "She's not a nice girl at all." They didn't know what Julia was really like. But still, Julia should not have left her like that; and they should never have got involved with breaking into someone's house.

Then she saw a police car driving past and her courage failed her. She dropped the package over a wall into a garden and ran away. Then she stopped. That was no way out. Mrs. Watkins would not get her treasures — whatever they were — if she left them there. She turned back and collected the package. She would take it home and later, when she could do it safely, she would go to the old lady's home and leave the package on the front step, knock at the door, and disappear before anyone could answer. In the meantime, she would hide it in her room. The trouble was her eight-year-old sister, Barbara, who shared her bedroom; she was a dreadful nosy-parker, always prying into things that didn't belong to her.

No one would be at home now, because her mother worked at the hospital on Thursdays. She would go and hide the package in her bedroom, find some place safe from Barbara's curiosity.

She hoped their neighbors wouldn't see her and wonder why she wasn't at school. She slipped quickly into the house, ran upstairs, and pushed the parcel under her bed to the far end against the wall. She was tempted to take the paper off and see what it was, but she was anxious about school. She should go back and get her mark for part of the day at least.

She ran to school and arrived, breathless, just in time for morning break. Only an hour and a half had passed and so much had happened. She had become a criminal — without intending to, but still, a criminal.

She went into the next lesson with her classmates, and no one seemed to notice she had been missing earlier; at least, no one commented until the afternoon, when her absence in the morning was drawn to her attention.

"I didn't feel well," she told her tutor, Mr. Harcourt.

"Miss Robinson wants to see you. Now," he said firmly. "I think you have some explaining to do."

16

How could she explain? She slowly walked to Miss Robinson's room in the older part of school. The old hall, with its wooden paneling and its Honors Board, was as it must have been for years, before the new part of the school was added. She paused to look at the Honors Board. Honors — she would never find *her* name there, she knew, not with what was on her conscience. She tried to thrust it to the back of her mind. The first date on the board was the year 1903 and beneath it several names: A. Johnson, G. Mayhew, R. C. Williams, and beside them the scholarships they'd won. That must have been when the school was just a girls' school. She wondered what school might be like without boys. She could do without the Joe Simpsons of this world, but she wasn't sure she would want to match herself only against girls.

She suddenly remembered she was to see Miss Robinson and tried desperately to think of some excuse for her behavior. She stood outside the room, gathering her courage, when, to her surprise, the door opened and Julia came out, smiling and self-assured. She did not speak to Mary, pretending not to see her. Mary watched her go and then turned as Miss Robinson said, "Well, young lady. What have *you* to say for yourself?" She looked rather pleased with herself as she waited for Mary to speak.

"Well?" Miss Robinson repeated. "Have you decided to follow school rules after all? I must say Julia made a handsome apology. What about you?"

"Yes, Miss Robinson," Mary said, but she didn't know what to say.

"You were very foolish dashing off as you did. I hope you see that?"

17

"Yes, Miss Robinson."

"Then we'll say no more about it. You should know, Mary, we have high hopes for you. You're usually such a sensible girl."

There it was again. Sensible. She didn't feel sensible. She felt stupid and wicked. Miss Robinson was still talking. "Most of your teachers speak well of you, especially Miss Taylor, in history. She tells me, by the way, that you think if the school has a new name it should be that of a woman."

Mary looked up. It had only been an idea. She hadn't thought seriously about it. "Yes," she said.

"I don't see why not," Miss Robinson said. "But none of our girls in the past seems to have done anything very notable, so the Thomas Wilton School seems to be it."

Mary turned to go, but Miss Robinson had another word for her. "You've got an important year ahead of you. Don't ruin your chances by doing anything foolish."

"No, Miss Robinson," Mary said in a whisper, but she felt she already had ruined her chances. She had done something foolish; she was a thief — there was no getting away from that.

She went to her class. She had been lucky to find Miss Robinson in a forgiving mood; at the very least she had expected detention. Perhaps her parents would not need to know she had missed school for a day and a bit. Perhaps her parents need never know what else she had been up to.

She became absorbed in her work and was glad the last lesson of the day was with Miss Taylor, when they were to discuss the personal projects each of them was to submit for the exam. There were so many interesting themes from

18

the period they were studying, but she was most attracted by the campaign that women organized to win themselves the vote. Julia had chosen to study changes of fashion and could not understand why Mary should bother her head about dry-as-dust politics.

"Women have got the vote, haven't they? So what's the use in looking back?" Julia argued. "Now, clothes are always interesting, always changing. And those dresses! Weren't they lovely?" She showed Mary some illustrations she had found, of ball gowns worn by actresses in 1909. They were beautiful, it was true, and Mary thought it must have been good to be alive then and able to dress with such style and elegance.

Miss Taylor made a note of what each member of the class wanted to research, advising changes here and there, suggesting books for study. When she came to Mary she said, "You've not chosen an easy subject. There's very little in any of our textbooks. Just a line or two. And it's too long ago, I think, for you to find anyone still alive who was involved in the campaign."

"How old would they be?"

"Ninety years old, at least, I suppose."

"I don't know anyone that old," said Mary and suddenly thought of Mrs. Watkins, but she wasn't as old as that. She was in her seventies, maybe, but not her nineties. She had a vision of Mrs. Watkins getting up slowly from the ground.

"Is anything the matter?" Miss Taylor asked. "Having second thoughts about your study?"

"No," said Mary. "That's what I want to do, the Votes-for-Women Campaign."

It was true, as Miss Taylor said, there were only one or two
sentences about the campaign in their textbooks and there
was nothing in the school library of much help. One name
was mentioned once or twice, a Mrs. Pankhurst, but there
was not a great deal about her. It seemed she was a "mil-
itant," a leader of the "Suffragettes"; there was mention
of window-breaking and of other sorts of protest, but none
of it really came to life as it was described, so that Mary
began to consider changing her ideas and choosing some
topic easier to research, like Julia's fashion. But she could
not change; it was important to her to find out how the vote
was won by women. She was not sure why, or how the idea
had come to her; she thought it was a chance remark of
Miss Taylor's: "No one ever *gives* people their rights; they
have to *claim* them."

"You're very serious," Julia said as they left school.

Mary didn't speak. She had not forgiven Julia for landing her in the mess she was in.

"What was in the package?" Julia asked.

"I don't know. I haven't looked."

"Where is it?"

"At home, under my bed."

"What are you going to do with it?"

"Take it back," said Mary. "Give it back to Mrs. Watkins.

Julia shrugged her shoulders. "If you want. I don't want
it."

"Why did you take it then?"

"For something to do," Julia said. "I was bored." She
moved away as her mother drove up. Mary looked after the

car. *She's not my sort,* she thought. *I don't know why I bother with her.* But she couldn't help liking her, in spite of the things she did. And it was no use blaming Julia for what had happened. She could have stopped her if she had thought quickly enough. She was as much to blame as her friend.

"You don't look at all well," her mother said to her when she got home. And she did feel rotten — not ill, but depressed and worried. She picked at her food and couldn't be bothered to quarrel with Barbara when her sister snatched the largest piece of apple tart.

"I think you're coming down with something," her mother said. "You've hardly eaten a thing."

"I don't feel hungry," she said. "I'll go up to bed for a bit."

Her mother looked at her with concern." I'll get you a hot-water bottle."

"Don't fuss, Mum," she begged. "It's nothing. I . . ." She wanted to tell her mother what she had done, but she couldn't. She knew she was going to burst into tears but managed to keep them back until she got upstairs and was lying on her bed. Then she wept. She didn't quite know why, except that everything was going wrong.

She woke with a start, wondering what had disturbed her. Then she heard Barbara getting ready for bed, bustling about, trying hard to be quiet but making more noise than usual. Mary pretended to be asleep, for she didn't want to talk, but she heard Barbara draw near her bed and was afraid she might look underneath it; there was no reason why she should but she was such an inquisitive thing.

21

Mary sat up in bed.

"I'm sorry," Barbara said. "I didn't mean to wake you. Mum told me to be quiet and I tried to be. Can I get you anything? A drink or something?"

Mary was sorry for having thought badly of her sister. She only wanted to help, it seemed.

"No. I'm all right. I don't know what's the matter with me."

"You look awful," said Barbara. "Really awful. I think you've caught something frightful." She moved away with exaggerated caution. "I don't want to catch it." She grinned impishly. "I don't mean it," she said. "But you do look rotten."

She didn't feel very good, but it wasn't that she had a temperature or a headache; she just felt miserable. But when Barbara started to chatter about some incident at school, she cheered up a little and thought sisters were sometimes quite useful in taking your mind off other things. She fell asleep while Barbara was still going on about her friends.

She woke in the middle of the night, suddenly afraid someone might have found the package. She got out of bed and felt about; it was still there, wrapped in paper, its secret intact.

"What are you doing?" She heard Barbara's sleepy voice.

"Nothing. Go back to sleep," she said and got back into bed. But her mind was so full of wild thoughts that she couldn't go to sleep herself. When she closed her eyes she could see Mrs. Watkins lying on the ground, trying to pick herself up. She had to keep awake because she knew if she slept she would dream of the old lady and she couldn't bear that. But, awake, she thought of her too and was upset about her. Perhaps she hadn't been able to get up. Old people's bones sometimes broke easily, she knew. She would have to go and see her, make sure she was all right, she must.

But in the morning when it was time to get up she felt worse, so that her mother said she would have to stay in bed. "I'll send a message to school that you're not well. I expect a day or two in bed will do the trick and you'll be better by Monday." She stuck a thermometer in Mary's mouth and sat beside her on the bed. "Well, that's all right," she said after a bit. "No temperature. I'm sure it's nothing serious."

Mary still didn't feel like eating and when her mother brought her breakfast, though she made an effort, she couldn't finish it. Her mother frowned. "You're not in any trouble at school, are you?" she said.

Mary shook her head.

"That nonsense about not wearing the school uniform is over, I hope."

"It's all right, Mum."

"I'm glad of that. That sort of thing is not worth getting into trouble for. There are more important things to worry about." She fussed about Mary for a few minutes, straightening the bedclothes, plumping up the pillows. "Have you got everything you want? Something to read? I've to go out for an hour or so, but I'll be back to make us some lunch. And you'd better find your appetite before then, young lady." She bent down to kiss Mary on the forehead and went downstairs. A few minutes later Mary heard the front

23

door close and her mother walking away along the street.

She threw the bedclothes back, got up and drew the package from under the bed. She unwrapped the brown paper to reveal a casket, made of ebony, its lid inlaid with a pattern of flowers in mother-of-pearl. She knew she had to open it to see what was inside, but she hesitated. It was not hers; it belonged to Mrs. Watkins and its contents might be very personal — love letters or a diary, and she felt she ought not to pry. But her curiosity was too strong. She slowly lifted the lid and, inside the satin-lined box, she saw a collection of things — papers, an old exercise book, a tie or something of the kind, frayed and worn, a couple of brooches wrapped in tissue paper, and some photographs. She felt guilty at having looked and closed the lid. These things were not hers and she had no right to look. She pushed the box back under the bed as far to the wall as she could. When she felt better she would take it back to Mrs. Watkins and beg her forgiveness.

She took a book from her shelves and tried to read, but her mind was full of the glimpses of the casket's contents. Why should anyone keep an old tie, one so worn? She remembered its colors: purple, white, and green, she thought. Or blue, white, and green? She had to look again to make sure.

She got out of bed again, drew the casket out, and opened it. Purple, green, and white. She had been right the first time. The tie was made of silk, worn at the edges. There seemed nothing special about it, so why on earth should anyone want to keep it? It must have some sentimental value, she supposed. And perhaps the papers she could see, letters in their envelopes, had sentimental value,

24

too. She would not look. They were private to Mrs. Watkins. But she saw that the stamp on one envelope bore the portrait of King Edward VII. That was before Mrs. Watkins's time, surely. She read the name on the envelope and was going to see what was inside it when she heard a key at the front door. Hurriedly she put the envelope back, closed the casket, pushed it back under the bed, got under the blankets, and was pretending to read her book when her mother came to see if she was feeling any better.

"You look flushed," her mother said. "Perhaps you have a temperature after all. Maybe I should call the doctor."

"It's nothing, Mum, honest." A doctor wouldn't be able to do anything for her. She didn't know who could. Only herself.

She did not dare to get the casket out while there was anyone in the house. She hoped her mother would go out to the shops or somewhere, but it seemed her mother didn't want to leave her on her own. She tried to tell her she was all right, but it was no good; her mother was concerned about her and especially her loss of appetite. She had made an omelet for their lunch, light and fluffy, and Mary would usually have enjoyed it, but today it tasted like blotting paper, and she could only take a mouthful and had difficulty swallowing even that.

Her mother looked at her with dismay. "What's the matter, love?" she asked. "You like omelets as a rule. There's nothing wrong, is there?"

"I don't know, Mum," she answered. "I just don't feel like eating. It makes me feel sick."

"What's wrong?"

Mary shook her head. If only she could tell her. "It's nothing, Mum, honest."

"I'm worried about Mary," Liz Thomson said to her husband when he came back from work.

"Isn't she any better? I'll go and see her when I've cleaned up." He was a decorator by trade and had been busy that day on an old building and looked tired and dusty.

"Perhaps she'll tell you more than she tells me," his wife said. "I think she may be in some sort of trouble at school."

"I'll see what I can find out. She might confide in me." And, when he was spruced-up and smart, he went into Mary's bedroom and tried to cheer her up and get her to say what was the matter. But he got nowhere. He went down to the living room, shaking his head. "She wouldn't say anything. Only said nothing was the matter. But there is something, I can see that. If she doesn't snap out of it over the weekend I'll call in at school on Monday and speak to someone there."

Mary waited until the family had settled down for the evening, her father and mother in front of the TV, her brother, Bob, tinkering outside with his motorbike, and Barbara busy with a complicated jigsaw puzzle that would keep her happy for a long time. Mary had gone downstairs for a few minutes but wasn't sorry to get back to bed. And, with everyone busy, she felt she could safely get the casket out and take a closer look at its contents.

She took out the envelope with the King Edward stamp. It was addressed to a Miss G. Mayhew. She thought the name was familiar but couldn't remember why. She sat on the bed holding the envelope in her hand, hesitating to open it. For a moment she felt as if the letter were addressed to her, as if she were Miss Mayhew. But she wasn't, she was Mary Thomson. Miss Mayhew, she expected, had died long since. Yet, holding the letter addressed to her, Mary felt as if Miss Mayhew was there somehow, herself uncertain as she took the sheet of paper from the envelope.

The paper had a printed heading: National Women's Social and Political Union, with an address in London. It was dated 28 September 1909 and read,

> *Dear Gladys Mayhew,*
>
> *I am sending you a brooch set with a stone which the Committee hope you will accept in memory of the stones you threw at the Government Stronghold on the 29th June last.*
>
> *Your courage on that occasion and all the other splendid work you have done in the movement is an example to other women.*
>
> *It is impossible to tell you how much we love and admire you.*
>
> *Affectionately yours,*
> *Emmeline Pankhurst.*

Mary felt tears welling to her eyes. She tried to brush them away but couldn't stop them. She had no idea why she was weeping for there was nothing sad about the letter and she couldn't help feeling a strange pride at reading it. But it was not addressed to her: she had no reason for feeling tearful pride; it was Gladys Mayhew who was loved and admired.

A sound broke into Mary's consciousness, footsteps on the stairs. Quickly she put the envelope and the letter back into the casket and shoved it far under the bed. Her mother quietly opened the door and peeped in at her.

"All right, my love?" she asked, and then, as she saw Mary's red-rimmed eyes, she exclaimed, "Oh my love, whatever is the matter?"

"I don't know," said Mary. "I feel so sad. But I can't explain." She would never be able to, for the feeling she had, mixed up with her own sense of shame, was a feeling of pride, of something secret to her and to someone else, someone she had never even known, someone called Gladys Mayhew.

Chapter Three

The next day, Saturday, Mary made up her mind to see Mrs. Watkins somehow. In the night she had dreamed of the old lady, who had been weeping about something she couldn't explain; and, when Mary woke, she had such a strong impression that Mrs. Watkins was in trouble that she knew she wouldn't rest until she had seen her.

She persuaded her mother that she was well enough to get up and go out.

"Some fresh air might do you good," her mother said. "But don't go too far and come straight back if you begin to feel tired."

It wasn't very far to the district where Mrs. Watkins lived. As she drew near it, Mary's steps began to falter. She wanted to know how Mrs. Watkins was but didn't dare to go to the house to enquire. She stayed for a while in the park trying to pluck up courage. It was no good. It would look too suspicious if she were to knock on the door and ask about the old lady.

Angry with herself for her cowardice she walked out of

the square toward the shops on the main road and saw Mrs. Watkins coming toward her, weighed down by shopping, a grocery bag in each arm. She stopped, put the bags on the ground beside her, rested for a moment, and then stooped to pick them up again. Without thinking Mary went to her and said, "Let me carry them for you."

The old lady looked up and smiled, her face wrinkling with pleasure, her eyes alert and interested.

"Oh, that *is* kind of you," she said. "Just the one, then. I can manage the other." But Mary took both bags and walked along beside Mrs. Watkins. "I do get a bit stiff these days," said Mrs. Watkins. "And I had a tumble the other day that didn't make things any better."

Mary felt guilty.

"I'm all right now though. It takes more than that to get me down." She walked up the steps to her front door and unlocked it.

"I never used to bother locking doors when I was just going to the shops, but it's better to be careful. Come along in then."

She hasn't recognized me, Mary thought, as she followed Mrs. Watkins along a dark hall to the rear of the house and the kitchen.

"Put them on the table, love. It's mostly cat food. Where are you, Murphy?" She looked around. "I expect he's found somewhere warm. He's getting old, like me. Doesn't move as rapidly as he used to." A large ginger cat, tail erect, appeared from a cupboard and came to rub against Mary's legs.

"There, he knows all about people. He's taken to you. That's because you have a kind heart." She took a can of the cat food and began to open it, but had difficulty with the can opener.

"Let me do it," said Mary.

She finished opening the can, forked some food into a saucer, and put it down for the cat, Murphy. Mrs. Watkins filled a kettle and said, "I'll make a cup of tea and you can tell me your name and all about yourself." She turned and looked closely at Mary, eyes intently studying her. "Sit down," she said. "What's your name?"

Mary hesitated. Why did she want to know? Had she recognized her? "Mary," she whispered.

"Speak up."

"Mary Thomson."

"Well, Mary. Carry this into the sitting room." She gestured to a tray which she had set with dainty cups and saucers and a milk jug. "I've got the best cups out for you. It's not every day I entertain a young person." She filled the teapot and, while Mary carried the tray, Mrs. Watkins carefully took the teapot and led the way to her sitting room. Mary looked about with interest. The furniture was old and well worn, the carpet had once been colorful but was now faded, and by the door the Hessian backing showed through the pattern. She remembered Julia's saying Mrs. Watkins was supposed to have a fortune hidden away. It didn't seem like it. Everything was neat and tidy but there was no sign of riches.

Above the fireplace, on the mantelpiece, was a row of photographs. She wanted to get up and study them, for several showed the costumes of Edwardian times; they would have interested Julia.

"Go and have a look at them," Mrs. Watkins said,

seeing Mary's interest. "They're my family, or my mother's family really. Bring them to me and I'll tell you all about them. That's if you're interested. I'm sorry. I'm an old woman. I don't know what interests young people. I don't suppose you want to know."

Mary got up and took one photograph from the mantelpiece. It was of a woman in her twenties, she supposed, dressed in blouse and tie and a dark skirt. She looked serious and intent. Pinned to her tie was a brooch, and her hand was touching it as if she wanted to draw attention to it.

"Ah!" said Mrs. Watkins. "I'm glad you chose that one."

"Who is she?" Mary asked, her curiosity growing as she held the photograph. She felt she should know the woman, but she could never have seen her.

"Do you really want to know?"

Mary saw Mrs. Watkins was gazing keenly at her, so that she wanted to drop her eyes, but instead she said, "Yes, I want to know. Please. Who is she?"

They were interrupted by a clatter from the kitchen. "Oh, that Murphy!" said Mrs. Watkins. "He must have smelled the chop I bought for my dinner." She got up stiffly from her chair and went to the kitchen, Mary following.

Murphy pretended to have nothing to do with the bag that lay on the floor. "You wicked cat," said Mrs. Watkins, picking the bag up and stroking him.

"I'd better go," Mary said, realizing she had been out longer than she had intended. Her mother would be worried.

"Oh," said Mrs. Watkins. "I'm sorry. I wanted to tell you about her. But I understand," she said. "Thank you for helping me. It was very kind." She opened the front door for Mary and watched her as she went down the steps. Mary turned and looked back. Mrs. Watkins looked a little forlorn but she smiled cheerfully and said, "Goodbye, then, Mary."

"Can I come back sometime?" Mary said suddenly, not sure why.

Mrs. Watkins beamed. "Of course, Mary. I should love to see you. Whenever you like."

Mary walked home and found her mother at the garden gate looking anxiously along the road for her. "You've been out far too long," she said. "You'll be tired." And Mary was suddenly without energy so that all she wanted to do was to lie down. She went upstairs to her room and, lying on her bed, she saw the young woman in the photograph on Mrs. Watkins's mantelpiece, almost as if she were there in the room with her. The vision was so real that Mary was about to speak to her when she realized she had been asleep. It had been a dream. That was all it could be.

Who was she? And why was she important? She must go back to Mrs. Watkins's sometime and find out. But she had a feeling that it might be dangerous. The old lady had looked at her very sharply once or twice. Perhaps she had recognized her and was playing some sort of game with her.

She didn't believe that, not really, for she had liked Mrs. Watkins, and she thought Mrs. Watkins had taken to her. She would go back as she had promised, whatever the danger. And somehow she must return the casket and its contents. It worried her to think it was there under her bed.

It *was* there, she supposed. She hurriedly got out of bed and felt under for it. At first she couldn't find it. But it was there, quite safe. She drew it out far enough to be able to open the lid and take out the tie. Then she heard footsteps and shut the lid, pushed the casket back as far as she could, got into bed, and pushed the tie under the pillow and lay back just as her mother opened the door.

"I thought I heard you moving," her mother said. "Ready to come down to dinner?"

But Mary didn't feel hungry. She shook her head. All she wanted to do was lie in bed.

Her mother looked at her with concern. "I thought you were feeling better. Eat something, please."

When her father came up with a tray and put it down beside her, she had a little beef and a few peas. He watched her as she ate. She wanted to tell him there was nothing the matter with her, that he shouldn't worry. But something *was* the matter. She knew what it was, that she was a thief, but she couldn't possibly tell him that, and if she did he wouldn't understand and would never forgive her.

"What is it?" he asked.

She choked on the food, wanting to tell him but not daring to. There was no one she could tell. No one.

Mary pretended to be asleep when Barbara came to bed, but her sister was determined to get her to talk.

"What's the matter with you?" Barbara said in a loud stage whisper. "I know what it is."

Mary sat up. "There's nothing the matter. Mind your own business."

34

"There!" said Barbara. "You've given it away. There *is* something wrong. You've been up to something."

"I've not been up to anything. You don't know what you're talking about."

"Dad's worried about you."

Mary was sorry she was causing her parents concern. There was nothing they could do to help. She would have to make an effort to brighten up, try to forget what she had done, and get back to normal.

It was easier thought than done. Sleep didn't come for a long time, long after Barbara was asleep, and even after the rest of the family had come upstairs and gone to bed. She tried to think about pleasant things, like the coming summer holiday they were planning, a camping holiday in Cornwall. She remembered the year before: it had rained every day, but that hadn't stopped them from enjoying themselves. That was when Bob first had his motorbike. He had ridden down on it, in spite of Mum's worries about him. It had all been fun. But he was not going with them this year, and Mary felt they would never be a family together again. It would not be the same without him.

She slept.

She didn't recognize where she was, for she had never been here before. The road was wide, and on either side were tall stone buildings, imposing and majestic, government offices of some sort. She heard someone at her side say, "Now's the time," and felt a nudge at her elbow. "Go on. Throw it. Throw it. Throw it." She raised her arm and heard a clash of glass, so sharp as to startle her into wakefulness, and leaving her puzzled as to what had alarmed her. For no reason that she could tell she felt frightened.

She heard Barbara stirring in her sleep, and knew everything was as normal. But she still felt uneasy, waiting for something to happen, something scary, something half-expected yet dreaded. She sat up in bed to break her dream and to make sure she was fully awake; she shook her pillow to make it more comfortable. Her fingers touched the tie she had hidden there and she took it in her hand, feeling the silkiness of it and the frayed edges. Somehow it comforted her and holding it to her she felt the peace of sleep steal over her, sleep undisturbed by dreams.

The next day was Sunday, and though she felt a bit easier in her mind she still had little interest in food. She didn't stay in bed but got up to do her Sunday morning chores. Usually she and Barbara shared the cleaning of their bedroom, but this morning she thought she had better do the job alone; it would be dreadful if Barbara found the casket and began to ask questions about it. Her young sister was never one to keep her mouth shut.

In the afternoon she was left alone in the house while her parents, with Barbara, went to have tea with Auntie Jessie on the other side of town, and Bob went for a ride in the country with his girlfriend. Her mother wanted her to go with them, but she said she had work to do for school, so in the end they went off and she was able to go upstairs and, in the quietness of the house, take out the casket and examine its contents. She still felt guilty at probing into it, but her curiosity could not be denied. She took out the letter to Gladys Mayhew from Emmeline Pankhurst and read it again. The dream of the previous night came back to her. She thought she had dismissed it from her mind, but there it was. The "Government Stronghold," that was what she had seen: government buildings, where she had thrown the stone. But of course it wasn't she; it was Miss Gladys Mayhew. She again felt something dreadful was about to happen just as she had felt in the dream.

She put the letter back in its envelope and took out one of the small tissue-wrapped brooches. She hadn't looked at either of them yet. The brooch was a pin of gold, with a small stone set in a claw, not a gemstone or any stone of value, but a piece of flint, rough-edged. She got the letter out again and read, ''I am sending you a brooch set with a stone which the Committee hope you will accept in memory of the stones you threw at the Government Stronghold.''

This was it, she had no doubt. This was the very brooch. And she had seen it before — in the photograph at Mrs. Watkins's. The woman in the photograph had been wearing it as a tie pin. Mary took the tie and saw two tiny holes in it. She opened the pin on the brooch and fitted it to the holes. They matched.

She knew then that the woman in the photograph was the Gladys Mayhew of the letter, the Gladys Mayhew who had thrown a stone at a ''Government Stronghold,'' the Gladys Mayhew who was ''an example to other women.'' Mary sat on the bed, holding the tie and the brooch in her hands, wanting to know more.

She sat for a long time like that, her mind wandering, but with moments when she saw again the buildings of her dream and heard again the shattering of glass, so real that she looked at her bedroom window half expecting it to be smashed, but when she shook her head to clear her mind of these strange images she saw that all was as usual. She went to the window, thinking someone might have thrown a pebble to attract her attention, but the street was quiet and deserted, with nothing to be seen except next door's cat, in the garden watching its kittens as they played together.

She turned her attention to the casket again and picked up an official-looking buff-colored form. The name of Gladys Mayhew leaped out at her.

> *Metropolitan Police*
> *"A" Division*
> *Cannon Row Station*

> *Take notice that you* Gladys Mayhew *are bound in the sum of* Two *Pounds to appear at the* Bow St. *Police Court situated at* Bow St. *at* 10 *o'clock* A.M. *on the* 12th *day of* July *19*09 *to answer the charge of* Committing Wilful Damage to Government Property *and unless you then appear there, further proceedings will be taken.*
> > *Dated this* 30th *day of* June
> > *One Thousand Nine Hundred and* Nine
> > *A. Godwin, Sgt.*
> > *Officer on Duty.*

Mary suddenly heard the sound of Bob's motorbike, the opening of the front door and Bob calling, "Anyone in?" She put everything back in the casket and went onto the landing to see Bob at the foot of the stairs, holding his crash helmet in his hand.

"Come down and make me a cup of tea," he said.

"Make one yourself," she answered.

38

"I've hurt my arm," he explained. "Go on. Don't be mean."

She went downstairs and made them both a cup of tea. She wondered if she could tell Bob about the casket, but he was no better at keeping a secret than Barbara. She glanced round at him. He was putting a Band-Aid on his arm.

"What've you done?" she asked.

"A graze, that's all."

They sat at the table together, not needing to talk, content to sit quietly, each filled with private thoughts, and Mary's were full of a young woman called Gladys Mayhew.

"Are you all right?" she heard Bob ask. "There's nothing wrong is there?"

"Why?"

"You're so quiet. You were such a long way away."

It was true. She was a long way away. In time and place. She was with Gladys Mayhew at Bow Street Police Court in July in the year 1909 waiting for sentence to be passed, and she was frightened.

Chapter Four

Mary went to school on Monday, though she didn't feel well. She had slept badly, waking from dreams that she wanted to forget. Barbara told her she had called out often in the night.

"You kept shouting 'I won't! I won't!' I'm going to ask Mum to move you out so I can get some sleep." But when she got downstairs Barbara was in such a rush that she didn't mention anything.

Mary could not remember shouting, but she thought someone had been trying to make her do something against her will. She couldn't think what it was.

When she got to school, she soon put the terrors of the night behind her. There had been trouble on the day she had been absent: Julia had been caught smoking and had been threatened with suspension again. Miss Robinson had been scandalized.

"She would be," said Julia. "But it took the wind out of her sails when I told her my mother didn't mind." Mary could imagine Miss Robinson's look of horror. "So she's asked my mother to come and see her. To talk about my behavior, she says!" She pretended to be unconcerned, but Mary could tell Julia was worried, in spite of her brave talk.

In the afternoon they had a double period of history, and Miss Taylor spoke about the projects they had chosen. She said she wanted them all to share in what everyone else was doing, and from time to time she would talk about one of the chosen subjects and get the whole class turning their minds to it. "However good anyone is — however much they know about their subject — they can always learn from those who know nothing."

"How can that be?" said Julia.

"Because those who know nothing often ask the most searching questions," Miss Taylor said. "Take Mary's subject." She turned to Mary. "How Women Got the Vote, isn't it? Now what do we know about it?" She turned to the class hopefully, but no one seemed to know anything. Nor did anyone seem to want to know.

Miss Taylor looked at Mary, but she didn't want to say anything yet, either. Miss Taylor smiled. "We'll leave that for now, wait until Mary has had time to work on it, then I'll set you all off thinking about it." Instead she talked about the South African War, which two of the boys had chosen to study. Mary's attention drifted. She wished she could ask Miss Taylor about the tie and the brooch and the other things in the casket. But how could she explain how they had come into her possession?

She didn't walk with Julia at the end of school for her friend was waiting for her mother and the dreaded interview with Miss Robinson. She would have liked to visit Mrs. Watkins, but she had a lot of homework to make up for her absence on Friday so she went directly home.

She stopped at the corner of the road, horrified to see a police car in front of their house. She wanted to run but instead she turned round and walked slowly away. They would have searched the house and found the casket and her crime would be revealed. She couldn't bear it; the mere idea made her feel sick again. As she got to the end of the road she looked back and saw a policeman getting into the car. He drove toward her and she turned her head away for fear of being recognized. He didn't notice her and drove off out of sight.

She did not know how she could face her mother, but it was pointless to stay out and a sudden flurry of rain made her mind up for her. She ran home and burst through the front door. Her mother turned to her indignantly.

"Why didn't you tell me?" she said.

Mary hung her head. How could she explain?

"It gave me quite a shock seeing a policeman at the door. I thought something dreadful had happened."

How could her mother take it like this? It *was* dreadful.

"And," her mother went on, "Bob should have known better than to keep it to himself."

"Bob didn't know."

"How do you mean, Bob didn't know? Of course he knew. It was his bike, wasn't it?"

Mary was puzzled, so she kept silent and let her mother grumble. "You knew about it. You should have told your father and me. Bob might have needed more than a Band-Aid."

42

She remembered Bob coming home with a grazed arm.

"Is that why the policeman was here?" she asked.

"What else would he come for? Someone reported the accident to the station. Luckily, it wasn't serious. But I'll have a word with your brother when he comes home from work. I'll have something to say about motorbikes. I've never liked them."

"It wasn't serious, Mum. There's no need for all this fuss."

Her mother looked incredulously at her. "You wait, my girl, till you have children. Then maybe you'll have some idea what a worry they are." She looked closely at her daughter. "And what about you? Did you have a proper school lunch?"

"Don't worry about me, Mum," Mary said, but she thought that if her mother knew what *she* had done, she would have even more cause to be upset.

She had so much homework that she had no time to bother about the casket, and when she went to bed Barbara was still awake so she had to curb her curiosity. She thought she would wait till her sister was asleep and then have a look, but the sleeplessness of the last few nights caught up with her and, before she knew it, it was morning, and her mother was calling to tell her to hurry or she'd be late for school.

She met Julia at the school gates. Her friend looked full of misery. Mary had never seen her like that before.

"What's the matter?" she asked. "What's Miss Robinson done?" She wondered what punishment had been decided. It couldn't have been suspension or Julia wouldn't be here.

"Not Miss Robinson," Julia said. "My mother." She seemed near to tears. "She's moving me next term, sending me to a better sort of school, she says. She doesn't like the company I keep here."

"Oh!" Mary was indignant.

"I know," said Julia. "She won't listen. I told her no one's to blame but me when I get into trouble, but she won't believe me. I hate her."

Mary was silent. She couldn't think what school would be like without Julia. She had other friends, but no one could take Julia's place. She wished there were something she could do.

"You're only a year away from your exams."

"That's what Miss Robinson told her."

"What did your mother say to that?"

"She said exams didn't matter, not for a girl. I thought Miss Robinson was going to throw something at her. I've never seen her so angry. I don't know how she controlled herself."

"What did she say?"

"She was speechless."

Mary shook her head in disbelief. Miss Robinson was never at a loss for words.

"It's true," Julia said. "All she could do was open the door and show us out. I felt awful." She looked suddenly so different from the devil-may-care girl Mary knew.

"I'm going to Miss Robinson, to apologize for my mother's behavior," she said. "I don't want the school to think I agree with her. I like it here. I don't want to go anywhere else."

*

44

As Mary walked away from school something puzzled her. At first she could not make out what it was, but suddenly it came to her. She knew why the name of Gladys Mayhew seemed familiar to her. It was a name among those on the school Honors Board. She went back to school, hoping none of the teachers would see her and ask what she was doing, and went into the old hall to look at the Honors Board. There it was, among the names under the year 1903, the name G. Mayhew. Was that her Gladys Mayhew? Could it be? She felt in her heart it was, but did not know how she could make sure. She did not dare ask Mrs. Watkins. Yet she had to know. Perhaps she had found a girl from the school who had done something memorable, perhaps even deserved commemorating in the name of the school. Then she thought again; throwing a stone at a ''Government Stronghold'' was hardly likely to be the sort of behavior approved by the school governors. She had to know more, much more.

Mary was unable to go to see Mrs. Watkins during the week for there seemed so much else to do. She had no chance to look into the casket for any length of time, with Barbara always near. But, from time to time, her dreams were invaded by a young woman. Mary could never see her face clearly enough to tell who she was. She knew it was a young woman, but she herself seemed to be going through the woman's tribulations and trials. And one of the dreams *was* a trial, in a police court, with a stern judge, a fierce male version of Miss Robinson. No one seemed to know what the charge was, but the evidence brought before the court was contained in a black box, inlaid with mother-of-pearl.

45

When Mary woke from this dream she knew what the charge was, and she knew she was on trial, and no one else. It made her feel sick to think of it, so that once again she found it difficult to eat and her mother again began to worry about her.

She pretended there had been some tummy-bug at school and she would be all right soon, but it was difficult to deceive her mother, who was always very sharp-eyed where the welfare of her family was concerned. However, there were other things for her mother to think of, like organizing for their summer holiday.

"I like camping," she explained to Mary's father, "but I would like a change every now and again, a holiday in a hotel with someone else doing all the thinking about meals. That's what I dream about."

"We're lucky to get a holiday at all," he replied. "Three more of my mates have been laid off this week."

Mary knew her parents were anxious about her dad's job. It would be awful to land more worry on their plate, so somehow she must keep the casket hidden, or get rid of it, or return it secretly to Mrs. Watkins.

She went to visit Mrs. Watkins early on Saturday morning, and was able to help her with her shopping. She saw how careful Mrs. Watkins was to choose the least expensive brands. All the shopkeepers knew her and asked after her health.

"I suffer from arthritis, you see," she explained. "And they all think I'm much worse than I am." But Mary saw she was glad to let her carry the shopping bags. When they got back to the house Murphy, the cat, welcomed Mary with a rub against her legs, and Mary felt quite at home, especially when Mrs. Watkins asked her to make a pot of tea for them both.

She did as Mrs. Watkins directed and took the tea tray into the sitting room. She went again to the mantelpiece and looked at the photograph. She knew the young woman in it, had shared in her dreadful experiences.

She wondered why she felt like that. What dreadful experiences? She knew nothing of her really, only guessed that she was called Gladys Mayhew.

"That was my Aunt Gladys, as a young woman," Mrs. Watkins said. "My mother's sister. You can see from the photograph she was a very determined young person. I was always a bit afraid of her till I knew her better."

Mary was quiet, frightened of giving herself away if she asked too many questions, but she longed to know more.

"Very determined," Mrs. Watkins repeated. "She was sent to prison two or three times." She seemed more proud than ashamed of her aunt's having been a convicted criminal.

"What did she do?"

"I'll show you something. It will tell you the whole story. I'm sure you'll be interested." She looked doubtfully at Mary. "*Would* you like to know about her? You're not just humoring an old lady, are you?"

"I'd like to know." Mary could not tell her how much she wanted to know about Gladys Mayhew.

Mrs. Watkins got up from her chair and went toward a cupboard set into the wall beside the fireplace. She opened the door and bent down to search inside.

"I'm sure it was here," she said. "You have a look, Mary. Perhaps your young eyes will be sharper than mine." She moved aside to let Mary look into the cupboard. "There should be a sort of box there, wrapped in brown paper. You can't miss it."

Mary pretended to look. She knew she wouldn't find it.

"I can't see it," she said.

"What did you say?"

"I can't see it. It doesn't seem to be there."

"It must be," Mrs Watkins said. "It *must* be." She was upset and, taking Mary's place, knelt in front of the cupboard, taking books and boxes out, until, tired, she had to stop.

"It's not there," she said. "I'm so sorry. I wanted to show you Aunt Gladys's things. But I can't. I don't know what can have happened to them. Oh my! It's dreadful. They meant so much to me. To think!"

She looked at Mary as they sat together on the floor, in front of the cupboard. "It must have been . . ." Mrs. Watkins began to say and then was unable to speak for distress at her loss.

"I'm sorry," she said. "I'm just a silly old woman. Give me a hand to get up." Mary helped her to her feet. "Pour the tea, there's a good girl," the old lady said, and sat in her chair, slowly shaking her head.

"I . . . ," Mary began. She had to tell her.

"What is it, my dear?"

"I'm so sorry," Mary said. "I . . ."

"It's no use pining," Mrs. Watkins interrupted. "Perhaps they'll turn up somewhere in the house. Maybe I've forgotten where I put them. And if they don't turn up I hope whoever has got them will cherish them for what they mean." She looked dreamily at Mary, as if she were seeing someone else rather than Mary.

"You know you have a look of her," she said. "Not really like her, but the same sort of determination. Are you a determined young woman, too? Lots of courage?"

"I don't know," said Mary. She felt anything but brave, merely ashamed of herself. She would go back home now, collect the casket, and return with it. She got up.

"You're not going?" said Mrs. Watkins. "Please stay a bit longer. I shouldn't ask, but I need your company. Just now. Just for a while."

Mary sat down again. She didn't want to go. She had become fond of Mrs. Watkins, although she didn't know much about her. She had such an open smile and such rosy cheeks; she must have been very beautiful when she was young; she still looked lovely. When Murphy came in and climbed up to Mary's lap, she knew she could not leave. The cat purred as Mary stroked him and Mrs. Watkins nodded with approval.

"You see, Murphy feels just like me. You're a welcome guest, a real friend."

They sat without speaking until Mary broke the silence. "Tell me about your Aunt Gladys."

"You really want to know?"

"I'm doing a project at school about Votes for Women." She stopped. What had she said? Had she given herself away? But Mrs. Watkins didn't seem to have noticed.

"Yes, that's what landed Aunt Gladys in jail. She was caught up in the campaign for the vote and nothing else mattered to her. It was her whole life for years. Nearly finished her life too. What do you know about the suf-fragettes?'' She looked sharply at Mary and Mary won-dered if she had guessed. ''No one seems to know anything about them nowadays,'' Mrs. Watkins went on. ''Women these days take the vote for granted. Some of them don't even bother to use it. After all the struggle to get it!'' A knock at the front door halted her.

''See who that is, Mary, would you?''

Mary went to the door and opened it. A policewoman stood there.

''Who is it, Mary?'' Mrs. Watkins called.

The policewoman called out, ''It's only me, Mrs. Wat-kins, WPC Collins.'' She went past Mary into the sitting room. Mary wanted to turn and run, but that would be cowardly and foolish.

''Will you bring another cup for Miss Collins?'' Mrs. Watkins said, and as Mary went to the kitchen she heard Mrs. Watkins say, ''She's a good kind girl. Saw me strug-gling with my shopping and came to help. Now we're friends. Aren't we?'' she said as Mary returned.

Mary nodded. She found it difficult to speak in the pres-ence of the policewoman, but she didn't need to for Mrs. Watkins went on. ''I've been telling Mary all about my Aunt Gladys.'' She looked at the policewoman with a light of mischief in her eyes. ''She was always on the wrong side of the law. Served more than one term in Holloway Prison. She went on a hunger strike, too.''

Mary glanced sideways at WPC Collins. She was pre-tending to be interested, but Mary thought her mind was on other things. She had taken her cap off and showed straight black hair. Her eyes were a pale shade of amber and very penetrating so that, as she turned to look at Mary, Mary looked away, suddenly afraid the woman could see into her mind.

"She wouldn't wear the prison uniform, you see, insisted on being treated as a political prisoner." Mrs. Watkins was looking hard at the policewoman, and Mary realized she was trying to shock her. But WPC Collins was unshockable, it seemed.

"That was a long time ago," she said. "Things have changed. I've come about those girls."

Mary had been sipping her tea. She put it down for her hands were trembling. The cup rattled in the saucer and Mrs. Watkins looked at her.

"Is anything missing?" the policewoman went on. "You said you weren't sure when you reported the incident."

"I don't think so," said Mrs. Watkins.

"And you've remembered nothing more about the girls?

Mrs. Watkins shook her head. "I didn't really see. It was all so quick. And I slipped and fell, so that all I saw was a flash of . . ." She stopped.

"Of what?" the policewoman prompted.

"No, it's gone."

"Young girls nowadays!" WPC Collins snorted indignantly. "You wouldn't believe what they get up to."

"They're not all bad," said Mrs. Watkins. "Mary here." She smiled, her whole face lighting up as she looked across at Mary. Mary reddened. She didn't deserve her trust nor her friendship.

"I must go," she said suddenly. "My mother will be wondering where I am."

"You'll come and see me again?" Mrs. Watkins said. "Please."

She nodded and let herself out at the front door, leaving the policewoman and Mrs. Watkins together. She wondered if they were talking about her. She was sorry in a way she had gone round to see Mrs. Watkins. She had almost given herself away. But she had found out more about Gladys Mayhew, not enough yet, but an idea was beginning to take shape.

Chapter Five

It was a fine June evening, with warmth from the day's sun still in the air, inviting them out. Mary was tempted to join her family for a drive into the hills, but she persuaded her mother that she had too much work to do to be able to afford the time to go with them.

"I expect we shan't be more than a couple of hours," her mother said. "It's a pity you can't come with us. You mustn't let your schoolwork get on top of you."

But Mary, though she had lots of homework to do, was more concerned to have time alone to be able to look into the casket. Two hours would make it possible to satisfy her curiosity. Then she could do as she intended, take it back to Mrs. Watkins and ask her forgiveness.

She went upstairs to her room, took the casket out from under her bed, opened it, and spread the contents on the eiderdown. She hadn't realized how much there was. Previously she had only been able to glance hurriedly at the stuff, fearful Barbara or her mother might interrupt.

The tie, the brooch with the stone, the letter from Mrs.

Pankhurst, and the summons to appear at Bow Street Police Court, she put on one side. She wished she could show them to Miss Taylor and get her comments but she didn't dare. She would never be able to explain how she had come by them.

There was a bundle of photographs, all of women, with signatures, names unknown to her, friends of Gladys Mayhew, she supposed. She put them aside. They would have interested Julia and helped her study of Edwardian costume, but she was not going to show them to her.

She examined the other brooch and wondered at its significance. She was sure that, like the brooch with the stone, this one had meaning. It was made of silver, and was in the shape of a portcullis, and had a broad arrow set on it. The arrow was enameled, with one prong colored white, one purple, and one green, the same colors as the tie — purple, white, and green. She knew there was some meaning to the colors; there must be, but she couldn't guess what it might be. She held the badge in her hand and sat staring at it, until her eyes glazed and she felt herself drifting off, losing touch with the reality of her bedroom, as if she were moving away to somewhere distant, unknown yet familiar, a place that held terror and suffering. She tried to escape from the feeling, wanted to cry out for help, but knew there was no help to be had. She could hear sounds of weeping, a scream, and she put her hands to her ears to shut out the sound.

The badge dropped to the ground and her eyes cleared, her mind freed of the horror that had threatened. The sound of weeping had gone and all she could hear was a cry of pleasure from someone playing in the street outside. Getting up, she went to the window and saw two boys kicking a ball, a woman with a baby in her arms gossiping to a neighbor. It was all so normal that Mary couldn't think why she had felt so disturbed a moment before. All that was left with her was the dying echo of a clang of metal, as if a heavy door had been banged shut.

She saw the portcullis badge on the floor, picked it up, wrapped it in the tissue paper again, and put it back in the casket. She picked up the tie and was surprised to find comfort in holding it. There was nothing special about it, it was frayed and worn, but there was something about it that made her feel as if she belonged.

Belonged? Why had that thought come into her head? And belonged to what? She didn't belong to anything except the drama club at school. She couldn't understand why such fanciful notions were taking hold of her. Everyone knew she was a "sensible" girl, and now here she was imagining all manner of things. But the feelings were there, however she tried to persuade herself she was being silly.

She put the tie down and picked up a hard-backed exercise book. There was nothing unusual about this, either, in outward appearance at any rate; it was the sort of book that still could be bought at any stationers. She opened it and a few sheets of coarse paper fell out.

"Oh!" she said aloud. "It's toilet paper." The sheets bore writing of some sort and when Mary looked more closely she recognized the signs as shorthand. The sheets were covered with the squiggles, so that every scrap of the paper was used. Here and there the pencil had scratched and torn the paper.

Mary, for the first time, regretted she had not taken the commercial course offered at school. She would have to ask Miss Forster, who taught shorthand, to read it for her. But of course she couldn't do that. Miss Forster was bound to ask questions.

She put the sheets aside, took up the exercise book, and began to read:

July 12–1909

We arrived at Bow Street at 10 o'clock. Were tried and sentenced. I got 1 month in the second division. We all said we would refuse to wear the prison dress or to obey the rule of silence. We all agreed. We left Bow Street in a Black Maria, 18 of us, each of us caged in a close airless compartment, bumping and jolting. Horrid.

Mary wondered what it meant. Gladys Mayhew was being punished for throwing a stone — that she knew, but why did she refuse to wear prison dress? And what was meant by the "second division"? She thought of how she and Julia had objected to wearing school uniform because it had seemed to make them look like inmates of some prison. How trivial that seemed to her now. She read on:

"Holloway." That must be the prison.

High forbidding walls, heavy doors. The wardress was very disagreeable. We said we wanted to see the Governor. At last he was sent for. "What's this," he said "a mutiny?" and refused to see us altogether, said he wasn't in the habit of receiving deputations.

Mary had a sudden vision of a man, pompous and proud of his authority, like their Headmaster. But Mr. Wardle

56

wasn't so bad really, just didn't know how to deal with girls.

I went in to see the Governor alone. When I told him we intended to rebel against all second division rules he said we could keep our own clothing & bags until he communicated with the Home Secretary, if we went to our cells quietly. We agreed.

Mary heard the sound of a car outside and thought the family had returned, but when she went to the window she saw it was their nextdoor neighbor. The woman with the baby was still at her gate talking, but the boys had gone. A vapor trail cut across the sky, a silvery arrow at its point moving into the far void. She turned back to look at her room. It was not a big room, but she and Barbara managed to share it without too many irritations. The wall above her bed was covered with pictures of pop stars. She would take them down tomorrow. They did not appeal to her now, and there were always others to take their place.

The women agreed to go to the cells. Gladys Mayhew, sentenced to one month in the second division, was in Holloway Prison. Mary tried to imagine what it must have been like to be in jail in 1909, to have a "disagreeable" wardress in charge of you. Here her room was cheerful and bright with color, with a window looking out to the world. She picked up the notebook and continued reading.

Was put in a cell. A little brown loaf, absolutely uneatable & a pint of cocoa was brought. My bed is a wooden platform raised about 4 inches from the ground which can be put on end against the wall when not in use, a mattress,

57

a pillow stuffed with horse hair, two sheets & a blanket made of woven string. It began to get dusk so I prepared for sleep when the door was flung open & the wardress announced the Doctor. He says "I understand you do not wish to be medically examined." I say "No." He departs. I'm in bed, which is not so bad, & it's about 8.30.

Mary heard a voice in the house below. She had been oblivious to the outside world. Her family had returned and she thought she could hear footsteps on the stairs. Hurriedly she picked everything up and piled it back into the casket, pushed it under the bed and was lying on the bed when Barbara opened the door.

"You missed a treat," her sister said. "Dad bought us all ice cream cones."

Mary shrugged. "I don't care," she said.

Barbara was disappointed at her reaction. "Mum says do you want a drink of cocoa?"

Cocoa? Her mind was still in the cell with Gladys Mayhew. Cocoa?

"Well," said Barbara. "Do you or don't you?"

Mary brought her mind back to her sister. "No, thanks," she said. "Not tonight." She could not face cocoa this evening.

She had difficulty getting to sleep, for whenever she was about to doze off her mind seemed to be filled with thoughts of Miss Mayhew. What sort of woman had she been? A woman of determination, Mrs. Watkins said. But what had she done for a living? Where had she lived? And, most important, where had she gone to school? Was she the G. Mayhew of the School Honors Board? She remembered

Mrs. Watkins saying that the campaign to win the vote had been her whole life for years. How could anyone be so devoted to a cause?

At last, weary with asking questions she couldn't answer, she fell asleep.

She woke. Her father was holding her to him. "What is it?" he was saying. "What's the matter, love?" Her mother came in with a startled look in her eyes. Barbara was sitting up in bed staring at her. "What is it?" her father said again, his voice filled with anxiety.

"Oh, Daddy," she said, unable to tell him. She didn't know what it was. She had been frightened, that was all she knew, and held tightly to her father. She had been threatened by someone, a woman who looked like WPC Collins only much more stern, a woman with black hair and piercing amber eyes.

Her mother felt her forehead. "You're hot, Mary." She turned to her husband. "I think she's got a fever. We'd better call the doctor in the morning."

"No!" Mary exclaimed. "I don't want to be examined."

"Why do you say that?" her mother asked.

"She's still in her nightmare," her father said. "Come along, love. It's all right. No one will touch you." He held her close and gradually the terror passed. Mary saw her father and knew she was at home, in her own bed, surrounded by her own family, and there was nothing to be afraid of.

"I'm sorry," she said. "Did I frighten you?"

"You were yelling your head off," Barbara said grumpily and turned over to sleep.

59

"Has it gone?" Her mother asked. "The dream?"

It had gone. But it had not been a dream. It had been real. She had been there in the cell with Gladys; she had been Gladys, for a moment, a moment of fear. She shuddered.

"You're getting cold, my love," her father said and tucked the bedclothes about her.

"I'll stay with her," Mary heard her mother say. "Until she settles again."

"I'm all right, Mum," she said sleepily. "I'm all right. . . ."

Mary's mother looked anxiously at her daughter. "Are you sure you're well enough to go to school?" she asked. "You had a very disturbed night."

Mary could only remember waking to find her father and mother standing over her. She tried to bring her dream back, but it was no use. It had something to do with Mrs. Watkins's Aunt Gladys, the young woman in the photograph. She remembered something about her.

It was the diary, the diary kept by Gladys Mayhew of her days in Holloway Prison, serving the sentence of one month's imprisonment. She had begun to read it.

After breakfast she went upstairs to her bedroom and had a quick look at it. It was there; she hadn't invented it. She wished she could take it to show to Miss Taylor, but she knew she could not do that.

"Are you going to school, then?" her mother called up.

She was tempted to pretend to be ill so that she could stay and examine the diary further, but she wanted to see Julia and she didn't want to miss her history lesson.

Julia was no longer just gloomy; she was angry. "I had

an awful row with my mother at the weekend,'' she said. ''I told her I wasn't going to change schools whatever she said.'' She looked at Mary. ''Is your mother as pig-headed as mine?''

Mary thought she was sometimes, but she wasn't going to admit it to Julia. ''Not like that,'' she said.

''And my father!'' said Julia with disgust. ''He didn't dare to open his mouth. Told me later I should do as my mother wanted. It would be easier that way. Easier!'' She was still fuming at morning break, but her behavior in class had been much better than usual. She had calmed down by the time they came to their double lesson of history and gave her mind wholeheartedly to the study of some fashion plates of Edwardian times that Miss Taylor had found for her.

''I've discovered a few references for you,'' Miss Taylor told Mary, ''but it's not going to be easy. I wonder if you should take some other subject.''

''Oh no,'' said Mary without thinking. ''I know where I can get lots of information.'' She stopped. How could she tell what she had found?

''Oh, that's good,'' said Miss Taylor. ''Where is it?''

''A Mrs. Watkins who lives in Cumberland Square.'' Mary had had to think quickly. ''Her aunt was a suffragette and went to prison for throwing stones at a Government Stronghold. It was in 1909.'' She couldn't stop herself talking. ''She was sentenced to one month in the second division for breaking a window, and she got a brooch for it from Mrs. Pankhurst.'' She suddenly realized how much she was giving away.

''This Mrs. Watkins told you all this? Would she be

willing to come into school and talk to us about it, do you think?''

"Oh, no," said Mary. "No!" She couldn't explain. Why had she said so much? Mrs. Watkins had hardly told her a thing.

"I'd like to meet her," Miss Taylor said.

Mary was horrified. She couldn't let them get together. They would want to know how Mary knew so much more than Mrs. Watkins had told her.

"Perhaps you could give me her address?" Miss Taylor was persistent and Mary didn't know what she could do to put her off, but luckily at that moment Joe Simpson threw a paper dart across the room and drew Miss Taylor's attention and anger.

Mary breathed a sigh of relief. She must be much more careful. That was the second time she had almost given herself away. But she found it very difficult to keep the thought of Gladys Mayhew out of her mind. She knew so much about her and yet so little. And she needed to know so much more.

When she got home she told her mother she had a lot of work to do and did not want to be interrupted. She got the diary out of the casket and opened it. Immediately she saw the figure of the young woman of the photograph on Mrs. Watkins's mantelpiece. There was no denying it; she was there staring at Mary from the pages of the diary, the diary she had somehow written in prison. Mary shook her head to dismiss the image of Miss Mayhew and it faded, but Mary knew she would only have to close her eyes to see her again, that small, serious-faced, determined, strong-willed, brave young person. Mary knew all these things about her were true, but she needed to know more. What was it that allowed her to face imprisonment with such courage?

And how had she been able to write a diary in prison? The writing in the book was so neat. She wished she understood more.

"Tuesday, 13–7–09," she read.

During the night there were screams from somewhere but I had quite a good night. The bell rang at a quarter to six & I washed in my pail as best I could. The wardress came in and told me to empty my slops. I rolled up my bed and tidied my cell. My No. is DX3 22. Breakfast came, a lump of that horrible brown bread and tea.

"Mary," she heard her mother call. "Time for tea."

She found it difficult to bring her mind back from Miss Mayhew's cell to her own house, difficult to bring herself to eat. But how lucky she was, she realized, as she joined the family for tea. She could even put up with Barbara's ways.

"What is it?" Her father asked her. "You don't seem to be with us. I think you're working too hard."

Mary shook her head in denial.

"Then something else is the matter. What is it, love?"

He would not understand if she told him so she said it was nothing, just that Julia Miller was going to be transferred to another school.

"That's good news," he said.

She glared at him and, without knowing why, burst into tears. "You don't know anything about it," she said. "She's my best friend." She wiped her eyes and controlled herself. "You don't understand, do you?" She left the table and stormed upstairs, aware that her mother and father were looking after her in disbelief. After a few moments her mother followed her.

"Dad didn't mean anything," she tried to explain. "It's just that all the teachers say you'd be better off without Julia to hold you back."

"They don't understand either," she said. "What do they know about me? What do you know about me?"

Her mother sat down on the bed beside her and put her arm about her shoulder. "What's the matter? You can tell me." She put her hand on the exercise book and moved it out of the way. Mary wanted to snatch it from her. How stupid she had been to leave it in view!

"There is something worrying you, isn't there, Mary? You've not been yourself for several days."

It was true. She had not been herself. She had felt like someone else. Perhaps she was someone else. That was nonsense, she knew. She looked her mother in the eye and said "There's nothing, Mum, honestly. Nothing at all."

She hated lying, but there was nothing else to do. Her mother would never forgive her for stealing.

"All right," her mother said. "But you can tell me, whatever it is. I'll understand."

Mary shook her head. No one would understand, not even her mother.

When she woke the next morning she felt refreshed. She had had no nightmares and for the moment forgot what had been worrying her. Then, "What's that?" Barbara asked, and Mary turned to see the tie, with its colors of purple, white, and green, sticking out from under her pillow.

"It's nothing," she said, gathering it up and stuffing it into her school satchel. For once Barbara's curiosity was easily satisfied, but Mary realized how easy it would be to give her secret away. She dreaded discovery. There was only one thing to do, somehow to get rid of the casket and its contents. She couldn't just throw it away. It meant so much to Mrs. Watkins. She must take it back to the old lady, own up to what she had done, and hope Mrs. Watkins would not take the matter any further.

"Hurry up, Mary. You'll be late for school," her mother called and hurriedly she got ready, had a hasty breakfast, picked up her satchel, and rushed off to school.

The first lesson of the day was with Miss Taylor. Everyone got down to work, but when Mary opened her satchel to take out her books the tie fell out on to her desk.

"What's that?" Miss Taylor asked, her voice alive with interest. "It can't be! I've read about the suffragette tie, but I've never seen one." She smiled at Mary. "Where did you get this? Your friend Mrs. Watkins?"

Mary was horrified. How could she have been so stupid as to bring the tie to school? She said nothing and Miss Taylor seemed to take it for granted Mrs. Watkins had let Mary have the tie.

"May I?" Miss Taylor said and reached out to pick it up.

Mary nodded, not trusting herself to speak. She could see Julia out of the corner of her eye shaking her head as if to say, "Don't give me away."

Miss Taylor went to the front of the class and held the tie up so that everyone could see. "Look at this, everyone."

"It's just a tie," Joe Simpson said. "Nothing special."

"Ah, but it is," Miss Taylor said. "Very special. Notice the colors. They were the colors of the suffragette women."

"Who were they when they were at home?" Joe Simpson said.

Miss Taylor directed a hard look at him. "You'll learn, my boy, when Mary has finished her project. I expect she'll tell you all about them. But look at this tie for now. The colors tell you a lot about those women." She turned to Mary. "Did Mrs. Watkins explain?"

Mary shook her head. She felt sick with guilt and fear.

"No?" Miss Taylor said. "The purple stands for dignity, white for purity, green for hope. When Mary has done more work on it, she'll maybe tell us more about the colors and how much they meant to the women who wore them." She looked again at Joe, who was scratching his head as if he found it all very puzzling. "Women!" he said under his breath but just loud enough to be heard.

"Yes," said Miss Taylor. "Women. Perhaps there was even a Simpson among them, maybe your great-grandmother." She smiled. "Who knows what your ancestors got up to?" She put the tie back on Mary's desk. "Don't forget, I'd like to meet your Mrs. Watkins sometime. And thank her for letting us see the tie. She must be very proud of it. I wonder if she has any other souvenirs."

Mary could not look Miss Taylor in the eye and pretended to busy herself with her notes. It was all getting out of hand. At every turn she was in danger, from Miss Taylor's interest in Mrs. Watkins, from Barbara's inquisitiveness, and from her own conscience. She glanced over to

Julia. Her friend was quite unworried, asking Miss Taylor some question about dress materials. Mary dropped her head in her arms and burst into tears. She felt a hand on her shoulders and looked up to see Miss Taylor, eyes concerned at Mary's misery.

"What is it?" she enquired.

"I feel rotten," Mary said.

That was it, she thought. She was rotten, wicked, and sinful.

"Go with her, Julia," Miss Taylor said.

"No," Mary said. "I don't need to go anywhere. I'm all right." *I'm all right,* she told herself. *I can deal with it. Whatever is the matter, it's of my own making, and I can solve it for myself.* "I'm all right," she repeated firmly. She took up her pen and began to write, hurriedly, almost without thinking, as if there were words inside her eager to escape onto paper. She wrote, unaware of Miss Taylor or Julia or of anyone else.

"I had to do it," she wrote. "I had to join the others and do something to show my feelings. Why can't they give women the vote? How can they ignore one half of the population? I deserve the right to vote as much as any man. That's why I broke the window, that's why I'm willing to go to jail. That's why I will never give up the struggle. You may lock me in a cell, threaten me, beat me, do what you will but I shall never give up the fight. No, not till we have won and the Cause is triumphant." In her mind she saw the face of a man, a tall, lean figure with stern forbidding features. "One month in the second division," he said and waved a hand to dismiss her.

She looked up and saw Miss Taylor standing in front of

her. "Mary," Miss Taylor was saying and her voice was soft as if coming from a great distance. "Mary," she repeated. "Are you all right?" Mary saw the rest of the class moving out of the room. She had not heard the bell for the end of the lesson.

"Mary."

"Yes, Miss Taylor, I'm all right," she said and followed her classmates. But she was not all right. She was in a daze, uncertain where she was or even, sometimes, who she was. She shook her head and caught up with Julia at the end of the corridor. Her friend took her arm and together they went to the science department for their next lesson. She was glad of the change. Perhaps it would clear her mind of thoughts of the suffragettes, Gladys Mayhew, and, most of all, of Mrs. Watkins.

Chapter Six

"Are you coming with us, Mary?" her mother asked. Her parents were going to a concert at Barbara's school.

"I've too much work," Mary said, delighted that she would have an opportunity to examine the contents of the casket without fear of interruption.

"You work too hard," her father said. "But I understand."

He didn't understand really, Mary thought as she watched the family leave the house. Even Bob had been persuaded to go to see Barbara perform.

As soon as she felt safe she went upstairs and took the casket from under her bed. Mrs. Watkins had been so upset at its loss that Mary couldn't help feeling dreadful at the thought that she had it here. *I'll take it back to her,* she said aloud, *but not yet.* She was curious to see what secrets the casket still held, what it could tell her about Gladys Mayhew.

Opening the lid, she stared inside. She was sure she had

left the diary on top, but it wasn't there. She took everything out and saw the exercise book at the bottom, beneath the collection of photographs. She couldn't remember putting it there.

"That nosy-parker Barbara," she exclaimed angrily. It was impossible to keep anything from her.

The anger went and instead, as she picked up the articles one by one, she felt a strange pride. The guilt and fear that had worried her before had gone. She took up the silver brooch, which showed the colors of the suffragette women, and she remembered what they stood for: purple for dignity, white for purity, and green for hope. She put the brooch down and searched among the papers. Julia would love to have the photographs of the women in their Edwardian clothes, but Mary felt they held more significance than that. Most of the photographs had signatures written across them, some with written messages of encouragement: "To my brave friend Gladys," "Be strong in the Cause," and "Courage, brave heart. Victory is sure."

Mary wished she could have shown the photos to Miss Taylor, to ask her about the women — three called Pankhurst, Emmeline, Christabel, and Sylvia, an Annie Kenney, a Constance Lytton, and others, all seeming to be such ordinary women in these posed studio portraits, but, Mary guessed, if they were like Gladys Mayhew, they were anything but ordinary.

As she was putting the photos back in the casket, she saw a sheet of paper at the bottom and picked it up. It was a letter, written in large, clear handwriting, but blurred here and there as if water had splashed on it — or tears she suddenly thought.

"My dearest sister," Mary read.

I wish I was strong and brave enough to do what you have done. I would never have the courage. I thought of you all the time you were in that horrid prison and prayed for you night and day. I think Mamma did too and even Papa, though they would not mention your name. I am so proud of you. I have told all the girls at school about you. Miss Henderson — you remember her — she is headmistress now — called me to her study and said I should not be proud of a sister who had broken the law. I told her it was a bad law which would not let women like her have the vote, and that you were my sister and I was proud of you whatever you had done. I don't know how I had the nerve. But she wasn't angry with me. Told me I was misguided and would learn one day. I think she secretly admires you. She mentioned you in our prayers in Assembly, asking for forgiveness for you.

I think of you every day. I wish I could do something too to help the cause. Is there anything?

Your loving sister Nell.

P.S. Papa does not know I am writing to you.

Mary put the letter back at the bottom of the casket and picked up the diary, turning the pages of the old exercise book.

Tuesday, 13-7-09
I am writing this after breakfast. There is a small win-

dow set high in the wall of my cell. By putting my chair against the pipes and standing on the back I can see to two yards and a church steeple and a bit of road outside. In one of the yards a black cat is sunning itself. Lucky cat! I've read all the rules. The books in the cell are a Bible, a Prayer Book, a Hymn Book & one called "A Healthy Home & How to Keep it." It tells me to take a daily bath and to sleep with open windows. Not much chance of that in Holloway!

I just looked out of the window again and saw prisoners at exercise. Poor wretches. They are wearing prison dress and walking round and round. I'm sure they must be dizzy. The Doctor came. I asked for more air. He said if we agreed to obey the rules and wear prison uniform we would be allowed exercise in the yard. I said "Of course we will not obey the regulations. We will not be treated as common criminals. We are political prisoners, have a right to wear our own clothing, and to have letters and books and writing materials." He seemed rather amused.

My tie is such a comfort and inspiration. It is delightful to have the dear old colours to look at when the walls seem to close in.

Mary could read no further. She put the diary down and went to her window to look out. If she wished *she* could get up, go outside, walk where she wanted, but she also felt imprisoned. She did not know why, but she shared with Gladys Mayhew the feeling of being hemmed in on all sides.

She saw a cat, a large black cat, lying on its back, rolling

72

on the pavement, enjoying the warmth of the evening sun. "Lucky cat."

She was beginning to understand things that had puzzled her before. Gladys Mayhew, imprisoned for breaking a window in protest against the treatment of women, was not a common criminal.

She, Mary Thomson, was. She could not deny it. She watched the cat sunning itself and was envious. Lucky cat, untroubled by guilt or an uneasy conscience.

On an impulse she put everything back into the box. She would take it to Mrs. Watkins now, own up to her folly, and ask the old lady for forgiveness. She wrapped it in its brown paper and left the house, determined to make amends. Mrs. Watkins was not the sort of person to bring the police in, she was sure. She would understand when Mary told her what had happened, but keeping Julia's name out of things.

She bent down to tickle the black cat's tummy as she passed. He purred and then rolled over, got to his feet and stalked away. *Lucky cat,* she thought again.

The roads were quiet, and she didn't see anyone she knew, but there were one or two people in the park, sitting on the benches, chatting together. She remembered how she and Julia had sat there. She glanced over to the terrace of houses, hesitating, wondering how she could explain things to Mrs. Watkins. But she had to go; there was no other way out.

She walked out of the park along the road and paused at the curb opposite Mrs. Watkins's house before crossing and then, suddenly afraid, drew back against the hedge as a police car stopped outside the house. From it emerged WPC Collins. The policewoman marched up the steps and rang the bell.

Mary turned and fled.

When the family came back Mary was in bed. The casket was tucked away, not this time under the bed where Barbara might look for it, but on top of their wardrobe, too high for her sister to reach, hidden from view behind empty suitcases.

Mary's mother was worried when she found her daughter in bed, but Mary said she was just tired. "That's all," she said. But it wasn't all. She was sick with fright. Had she said something to give herself away when she last visited Mrs. Watkins? She tried to think but couldn't; her mind was full of confused images, jumbles of conversation, sudden flashes of pictures of prison walls, of a small cell, of a window set high in the wall, of trying to peer out to see what was going on in the world outside and seeing only women in brown uniforms, women and then girls, herself and Julia, walking round a prison yard, round and round until they were giddy and fell down. The other girls walked past and ignored them. Miss Taylor came and looked down at them and smiled and said "They were always as thick as thieves, those two."

"Mary. I've brought you some cocoa. Take it. You'll feel better. You look dreadfully pale." Her mother looked at her with concern. "What's the matter, love?"

She wished she could say, but she couldn't even explain to herself all the emotions that were tumbling through her, shame and pride, guilt and fear, courage and weakness, need to be comforted, and determination to show independence.

"What is it, Mary?"

She shook her head. Even if she knew she couldn't tell. She raised her eyes to look at the wardrobe, anxious to make sure the casket was safely hidden. Her mother stood up to see what it was that interested her daughter.

"I'm going to be sick," Mary exclaimed and her mother turned quickly to her to help her to the bathroom.

It was not a trick, she told herself, for she really was sick. She looked wanly at her mother, washed, and went back to bed.

"If you're not better in the morning I'll stay off work and call the doctor," her mother said.

"I'll be all right. I expect it was school lunch." She felt sleepy. "That awful brown bread," she muttered.

"Brown bread?" her mother said. "Whatever do they feed you on at that place?"

But Mary was asleep. Her mother stroked her hair away from Mary's pale face, held her hand to her daughter's forehead for a moment, shook her head in puzzlement, and turned the light off.

"Are you sure you're fit to go to school?" Mary's mother asked anxiously. "You don't look your usual self."

I'm not my usual self, thought Mary, but she said, "I'm fine. Don't worry." She couldn't bear to stay at home to brood, to be all by herself, confined to her small room, imprisoned there by sickness.

"Don't worry. I'm OK."

"Come straight home if you don't feel well and I'll call the doctor."

Mary needed to go to school. Perhaps there she could forget all about Gladys Mayhew and Votes for Women and Mrs. Watkins; there, she could try to put prison out of her mind. She didn't even have a lesson with Miss Taylor to bring it all back. Her timetable today was filled with French and math and home economics.

Julia helped her to forget, for she was full of her own troubles.

"I'm going to leave home," she announced. "I told my mother I wasn't going to move schools. She can do what she wants, but I'm not going to that school she talks about. It's nothing like as good as this. Only girls there for a start, would you believe?"

"And what did your mother say?" Mary asked.

"She wouldn't listen. Told me I might be taught manners there, learn to do as I was told." She shrugged her shoulders. "She doesn't believe me, but I'll leave home, she'll see. She can't stop me."

"Where would you go?"

Julia shook her head uncertainly, so Mary took her arm and together they went into class.

The first part of the morning passed quickly, and Mary was able to concentrate on her work, but in an idle moment just before morning break she glanced out of the window and was horrified to see Policewoman Collins walking into school. She turned to Julia, and then away again. She must remember to keep her friend out of this. She must take the blame all to herself.

She was not surprised when a knock came at the door and a message was brought in. She knew what it would be. Mr. Bryson, the teacher, looked over to her and said, "Miss Robinson would like to see you at the end of the lesson, Mary." She thought he looked at her with suspicion; she thought the whole class looked as if they knew all about her. She pretended to be unconcerned when the bell rang, and she walked along the corridor to Miss Robinson's room as if she hadn't a care, but her heart beat fiercely and her knees shook. She had never felt so terrified. Again, she felt sick, but she conquered it; she was tempted to run out of school and escape, but she knew there *was* no escape. She must face up to whatever fate — or Miss Robinson — had in store.

Miss Robinson was at her door, keeping a watchful eye on the passing pupils. "Go in, Mary," she said. "Policewoman Collins wants a word with you. I'll join you shortly." She turned to rebuke Joe Simpson who was roughly pushing his way past a slow-moving group of girls.

Mary hesitated. "Go in, girl," Miss Robinson said impatiently.

Mary went in; Miss Collins, smart in her dark blue uniform, stood with her back to her, looking out of the window onto the schoolyard. When she turned round her face was in shadow so that Mary couldn't tell what she was thinking. She didn't speak either but waited for Miss Robinson to join them. Mary stood still, staring in front of her.

"Right." Miss Robinson came in, closed the door, and sat at her desk. "Switch the light on, Mary please. It's gloomy in here. That's better. Now we can see each other. You've met Miss Collins, I understand, Mary."

Mary looked at Miss Collins and nodded. The police-woman smiled and Mary felt a moment's relief. Then Miss Collins said, "Mrs. Watkins." Mary's heart missed a beat; she clasped her hands in front of her, nails digging into her palms to keep from crying out with shame. She lowered her eyes.

"I went to see her yesterday," Miss Collins went on and turned to Miss Robinson in explanation. "She's a dear old soul, lives on her own, no family except in Australia, nothing but memories, until Mary came into her life."

I stole those memories, thought Mary. She looked down at her feet, trying to hide her fear.

"She's very fond of you, Mary," Miss Collins went on. "She looks forward to seeing you. You've made a big difference to her. I promised I would find you and let you know that she missed you last week when you didn't come to see her. It was easy enough to find you." She turned to Miss Robinson. "The school uniform is very distinctive, so I knew where to come."

Miss Robinson smiled at Mary. "I'm so glad you have time to spend with her. There's more to life than discos, you know, and more to life than homework, come to think of it. How did this Mrs. Watkins come to your notice, Miss Collins?"

"A couple of girls broke into her house some weeks ago, and she thought she ought to report it."

Miss Robinson smiled again at Mary. "I'm glad our girls aren't like that. Well, Mary, you've obviously made a good impression on this Mrs. Watkins. I hope you will do as Miss Collins says and keep in touch with her. And if the school can do anything, let me know."

"You'll visit her, Mary?" Miss Collins said. "She would like to be able to rely on you. She doesn't expect much, just to call in and spend a few minutes with her every now and then. You'll do that, Mary? She's very fond of you."

Mary nodded and swallowed as she tried to speak. She liked Mrs. Watkins, too; she would go to see her that very day.

"Don't let her down, Mary," Miss Robinson said. "Your visits obviously mean a great deal to her."

Julia was waiting for her. "What did the battleaxe want?"

"Nothing special," Mary said. She couldn't share her thoughts about Mrs. Watkins with anyone, not even Julia.

Mrs. Watkins greeted her warmly. "I've missed you," she said, " and so has Murphy, you see," as the cat rubbed himself against Mary's legs. "Come in, sit down, and have a biscuit and a cup of tea. You know where the things are." She seemed delighted to see Mary and cleared some papers off the table so that Mary could put the cups and saucers there. "I've been sorting some papers out," she said. "I thought I might have some things about my Aunt Gladys. You seemed curious about her before." She looked at Mary uncertainly and said, "I'm a foolish old woman to think you might be interested in the past. I'm sorry. Don't bother your head about me."

"No," said Mary. "I *am* interested, really, I'd like to know all about her."

Mrs. Watkins reached up to the mantelpiece for the photo of her aunt and handed it to Mary. The young woman with the determined jaw and the clear eyes gazed steadily out of the frame at Mary, and Mary looked back, seeing so much more than was in the photograph. Gladys Mayhew — she knew her, better almost than she knew anyone else, had shared a cell with her, looked into her mind, seen her fears, and knew her courage.

She looked up from the frame to see Mrs. Watkins's eyes staring into hers.

"What have you seen?" the old lady asked.

"So much," Mary whispered.

"There's so much to see, so much to tell." Her voice faded away and her eyes seemed to be looking beyond Mary into the distant past, maybe. Mary was silent, waiting.

"Have your tea," Mrs. Watkins said briskly. "I mustn't keep you. I'm sure you have lots more to do than spend time listening to me. But you'll come again, won't you? Perhaps at the weekend when you have more time. You don't mind?"

"I want to know all there is to know about her, about your Aunt Gladys, I mean."

"Then I shall tell you. Next time."

"You look a lot better than you did this morning," her mother said when she got home. "I was quite worried about you."

"There's no need," Mary said. "I'm fine." And for the present she was.

Chapter Seven

"Mrs. Watkins would like to be able to rely on you," the policewoman had said. But Mrs. Watkins wouldn't trust her if she knew what Mary had done. Mary couldn't let her know. She must keep her respect, though she knew she didn't deserve it.

She could never admit she had stolen her precious mementos of her Aunt Gladys; she would have to find a way of returning them secretly, put them somewhere in Mrs. Watkins's house, and then "by accident" find them for her. Yes, that's what she would do, but she'd have to bide her time, wait until Mrs. Watkins took her visits for granted.

Besides, she wanted to keep the casket with its contents a bit longer. They brought her nearer to Gladys Mayhew, and that was all that mattered to her just now.

She was impatient to read more of the diary, but had no chance; some member of the family was always about. Barbara hadn't spoken of it, so Mary began to think she'd been mistaken in believing her sister had pried into the box and moved the diary. She must have moved it herself, for there were times when, reading the diary, she seemed to lose possession of herself, when she couldn't quite remember what she had said or done.

She told her mother a little about Mrs. Watkins but didn't say how she had come to know her, explained only that she had volunteered to visit her when Mrs. Watkins's name had been mentioned at school.

Her mother was pleased. "And you must bring her to see us sometime. Invite her over for Sunday lunch. I'm sure she would like that."

Mary didn't answer; she wasn't sure she wanted Mrs. Watkins to meet her family, not yet, not until she had cleared her conscience.

She went to see Mrs. Watkins on Saturday and helped her with her shopping. Then they sat together quietly for a while. Mrs. Watkins seemed tired, and Mary didn't want to disturb her, but there were a lot of questions she wanted to ask — about Gladys's sister Nell, for example. But she didn't dare to speak about her, for how could she explain that she even knew of Nell's existence?

Mrs. Watkins's eyes were closed and Mary got up as silently as she could so as not to wake her.

"It's all right," the old lady said. "I wasn't asleep, just thinking. I found some photographs that might interest you. They're on the table. Bring them here. You must tell me, though, if you get fed up with my memories. And when I've finished my chatter you can tell me all about yourself."

Mary went to the table and picked up a cardboard box overflowing with photographs of all kinds.

"The old ones are on top. Let me see." Mary handed her the box, and Mrs. Watkins picked up a photograph and sat staring at it before passing it to Mary.

Just a photograph of a girl about Mary's age, face and shoulders, with the hair parted in the center and caught in braids, one on either shoulder; there was a strong resemblance to Gladys Mayhew, but without the determined jaw and the intensity of stare. This girl's eyes looked dreamy, thoughtful, perhaps the result of careful posing by the photographer, but Mary thought it was natural to the girl.

"Nell," she whispered to herself.

"What did you say?" Mrs. Watkins asked.

Mary looked up startled. Had she said the name aloud? "Who is it?" she said hurriedly. "She's very pretty."

"Yes, she was, until the day she died." Taking the picture from Mary, she sighed. "My mother when a girl," she explained and put the photo aside and reached for another.

"What was her name?"

"My mother? Helen, Nell to her friends and family."

"Was she . . . ? Did she . . . ?" Mary was afraid to ask too many questions for she was sure she would give herself away. But Mrs. Watkins seemed to know what she wanted to ask.

"You mean was she a suffragette like her sister Gladys? She didn't go to prison or anything like that, but she used to sell the women's paper on the streets. 'Votes for Women' it was called." She picked up another photograph. "This should interest you."

It was of a small group of girls, all dressed in blouses and ties and long skirts. They were standing in front of a building, a building that Mary thought she recognized. She looked up at Mrs. Watkins.

"Yes," Mrs. Watkins said. "That's your school. At least it's the old part of your school. Aunt Gladys was a pupil there."

"I knew it," said Mary softly to herself. "I knew it."

Mrs. Watkins did not seem to hear her and handed another photo to Mary, a snapshot of a man and woman sitting in deck chairs on a beach, looking self-consciously at the camera. "My grandparents — the only picture I have of my mother's parents. I never knew them. There's something written on the back. What does it say?"

Mary read the penciled note. "Bridlington, July 1909," she read aloud.

"I suppose that was a family holiday. I expect my mother took the photo. Gladys wouldn't be there of course. She was in prison. That was her first time."

"First time?"

"Oh yes. She was sent to prison three times. The second time was the worst."

Mary waited for Mrs. Watkins to go on, but she said nothing more, merely sat looking into her past, as if she had forgotten Mary was there.

"What was I saying?" she said at last.

"The second time she went to prison."

"You don't want to know." She seemed reluctant to say anything more.

"What happened?"

"Some other time. Not now." She got up stiffly and went into the kitchen. Mary followed. Mrs. Watkins filled

84

the kettle and put it on the gas ring. "They were brave women, even if misguided," she said, shaking her head. "It was terrible for their families, knowing what was happening to them. My mother never forgot." She looked in Mary's direction but didn't seem to see her. "She admired her sister, and when she saw her. . . ." She stopped, looked at Mary, and said, "Brew the tea, Mary. I'm parched."

"But," said Mary.

"Not now," Mrs. Watkins interrupted. "I'll tell you one day, but not now." She went back into the living room, gathered the photos together, and put them back in their box, sipped her tea, and said, "Now it's your turn, Mary. Tell me about yourself and your family."

"There's nothing to tell," Mary said.

Mrs. Watkins laughed. "There's always something. Families are interesting. To me, anyway. You have a family, haven't you? Brothers, sisters?"

"One of each," Mary said, but she didn't want to talk about them. There was nothing interesting about Barbara and not much about Bob that was worth telling.

"I expect they're all right, really," Mrs. Watkins said, seeming to understand Mary's unwillingness to talk. "And your mother and father?"

"They're all right," Mary admitted.

"You must thank your mother for letting you come and keep me company. Perhaps you'll bring her round to see me so that I can thank her myself for having such a lovely daughter."

Mary felt awful at her deceitfulness. She didn't feel the

least bit "lovely." "I'd better go," she said.

"You've brightened my day," Mrs. Watkins said as she showed her to the door. Then, as Mary said goodbye, the old woman began, "How did you . . . ?" but let Mary go without finishing the question.

Chapter Eight

Mary watched as Barbara went off along the street. She saw Bob straddle his motorbike and set off in the other direction. She could hear her mother and father talking downstairs. They wouldn't interrupt her, would think she was getting on with her homework.

She got the box from the top of the wardrobe, took out the diary, and began to read from where she had left off before:

There are more women exercising; they are dressed in brown. The boots are huge and the clothes most degrading. The Matron is very severe. The wardresses so far have been quite decent . . . . The doors are unlocking again. I wonder what it is now. Dinner! A tin of broth with a lot of pearl barley in it, & potatoes & the usual lump of bread. Finished dinner (ate the potatoes and about 6 spoonsful of broth). I mounted my chair with shoe in hand. We all knocked through to each other and commenced operations. I smashed 3 panes. Wardresses came running. One white with rage bursts into my cell . . . . All is quiet now.

Oh! for a good square meal to eat! Just looked out of the window and saw three painters below. They saw me & smiled. I pushed my purple, white, and green tie through the hole in the window and waved it to them. A wardress appeared below so I disappeared.

She was watched all the time through the inspection hole in the door, she'd stuffed paper into it so that she could have some privacy, but a wardress rushed in, pulled the paper out, and flung it away. "Every time you cover it up it will be uncovered." Bang went the door.

Mary looked about her as if she, too, were under observation. She went to the window. Their nextdoor neighbor, Mr. Meadows, was up a ladder painting the window frames. He saw her and waved. She waved back at him. He said something and she opened the window to hear him.

"Lovely day," he said.

"Yes," she said. She left the window open. She needed to feel the fresh air, needed to know she could get up and move about and go outside whenever she wanted.

I have pulled my belt to the tightest hole. More unlocking doors. Jangling keys. Voices. A wardress came to count the number of panes I had broken. I read until teatime or is it supper? I used my knife to scratch my name and Votes for Women on the plate. Tea consisted of the usual loaf, I could only manage a few crumbs it is so vile, and a pint of water as I refused the cocoa. My fat will soon be reduced.

Mary heard someone call and then her mother's footsteps on the stairs. Hurriedly she hid the diary under her pillow.

"Didn't you hear me, Mary? It's tea time." Her mother appeared at the door. "Come on, love."

She went downstairs and saw that her mother had prepared a salad. It looked delicious, but Mary didn't feel hungry. She must make herself eat. She didn't want her mother to ask her questions or make a fuss. She forced the salad down but couldn't touch the bread. She saw her father looking at her with concern, but he said nothing.

It was all so complicated.

Mary stood in front of the Honors Board in the old school building. There it was: 1903 — G. Mayhew, her Gladys Mayhew she knew now, someone from the school who had been different, who had in some sort of way made a name for herself, perhaps in a strange way, but a name that should be remembered. Perhaps hers was the name the school ought to bear. But how could she persuade people of that? No one else had ever heard of her. She became aware that someone was standing by her. It was Miss Taylor. "Something interesting?" she asked.

Mary was not ready to tell her. "Not really," she said and made an excuse to get away.

She went to see Mrs. Watkins straight after school. She knew her mother wouldn't mind — she had encouraged her to go, for it was almost a week since she had gone last.

"I've found one or two things that will interest you, I'm sure," Mrs. Watkins said. "But the most interesting things were in the stolen casket." She looked at Mary. "I hope whoever's got it appreciates its meaning. Do you think they will, Mary?"

Mary didn't know what to say.

"Anyway, I've found a letter that Aunt Gladys wrote to her sister Nell, my mother. Perhaps it will help you to understand why she was willing to face the most awful indignities."

"Indignities?"

"The things that happened to her in prison. How could such a nicely brought-up young lady go through so much?" She held out an envelope to Mary. "It's in there. Treat it carefully. I don't want to lose that as well."

There were two sheets of paper in the envelope. She had seen the writing before — in the diary. She looked up guiltily to see Mrs. Watkins gazing intently at her. "You sit down and read it while I make the tea," she said.

The letter was dated in November 1909. "My dearest Nell," it began.

I am sorry you had to see me before I had time to get better. You mustn't cry. I shall soon fill out and make up my lost weight. I am being well looked after in London at a nursing home run by our friends. I shall come to see you as soon as I am able. Tell Mother and Father I am sorry to have caused them such distress, but I am not sorry for what I did.

You must understand, Nell, that our Cause is right. I do not always like what I have to do but unless women are prepared to show their anger at being left out of affairs no one will take any notice of them.

I know you want to help the Cause and I am glad but I do not want you to suffer like me. Keep out of trouble dearest. I could not bear to think of your having to go through the same as me. The hunger was bad enough, but

*worse was the wardresses and doctors forcing food down
me. I cannot tell you of the pain and humiliation of it. I do
not want that to happen to you. Promise me you will not
do anything to risk it.*

*But I shall go on. I have to. It is enough that one of us
should fight in this way. There is no need for you to be
treated as I have been. You are too young, too delicate,
and too dear to me.*

Your loving sister Gladys.

Mary looked up to see Mrs. Watkins holding out a cup
of tea to her.

"My mother never forgot how her sister looked when
she came out of prison that time. She told me about it when
she thought I was old enough to understand."

"I don't understand," said Mary.

"No. It's difficult now when women have won the right
to vote. We take it for granted. And it's so long ago. But
not for me, and it should not be for you." She sat down and
took the letter from Mary's hands.

"She was a brave woman. And quite tiny. How tall are
you?"

Mary shrugged her shoulders. "Five feet four, I suppose."

"Taller than Aunt Gladys by three inches. A bit of a
thing, she was. But tough. She had to be."

"Why did she have to be made to eat? It sounds horrid."

"It *was* horrid. You must know that these women were
demonstrating for what they regarded as their natural right,
the right to vote. They had done everything they could
within the law to persuade the government of the justice of

91

their case. When they broke the law they claimed they should be treated as political prisoners — given First Division status, it was called. And when they were refused that, they went on a hunger strike, would not eat. At first, after a few days of that, they were released from prison, but when they were imprisoned later and again refused food the Government decided to force it down them.''

''How?''

''It was barbarous. They were held down by wardresses while two doctors forced a tube up a nostril. Then a mixture of brandy and milk was poured into a funnel and down the tube. You can imagine how they felt. Some of them became very ill afterward and were damaged for life.''

''And this happened to Gladys Mayhew?''

Mrs. Watkins gazed into Mary's eyes. ''Yes, it did, but I told you she was tough. She survived and never stopped fighting, even after women got the vote. She said there was always more to do, more rights to be won.'' She had brought some iced buns with the tea and held out the plate to Mary.

''No, thanks,'' said Mary. ''I couldn't.''

Mrs. Watkins smiled. ''There's no need for you to go on a hunger strike, you know. And I made them specially for you.''

Mary took one though she did not feel like eating. But it was tasty, and she finished it and took another when Mrs. Watkins offered her the plate.

''We shouldn't forget women like my Aunt Gladys,'' she said. ''Even if they were sometimes foolish.''

''Foolish? I thought you admired her.''

''Of course I admired her, for her courage, but I don't

know that she was always the most sensible of women."

Sensible — that word again, thought Mary.

"Anyway," said Mrs. Watkins. "Enough of me and my family. What about you and yours?"

There was nothing Mary could tell her, nothing that seemed of any interest or importance.

"Or your friends?" said Mrs. Watkins, looking straight at Mary.

Mary was silent, couldn't even mention Julia's name, thinking of how she had called Mrs. Watkins an old cow and how she had behaved.

"No one special," she said.

"That's a pity," said Mrs. Watkins. "Friends *are* special. I thought . . . . ." She stopped. "I'd better let you go. Your mother will be wondering what you're up to."

Mary's mother met her at the front door. "Your friend Julia is here," her mother said. "She's upstairs in your room. She seems very upset."

Mary rushed upstairs. Julia was standing at the window of the bedroom looking out to the road. She turned when she heard Mary come in. Her eyes were puffy and red, but her mouth was set in a firm, defiant line.

"What's the matter?" Mary said.

"I've left home." She pointed to a suitcase at her feet. "I came to say goodbye."

"But where will you go?"

"I don't know. Anywhere to get away from my mother. She doesn't care what happens to me, anyway. She'll be glad to see the back of me. She told me so."

"You can stay here," Mary said impulsively.

93

Julia shook her head. "Your mother doesn't want me."

"I'll persuade her. She'll understand." Mary looked at her friend. "You'd better do something about your face. You look awful. The bathroom's next door. I'll go and see Mum." She found a towel for Julia and left her staring at herself in the bathroom mirror.

"What's the matter with her?" Mary's mother asked.

"She wants to stay overnight."

"Why on earth should she do that?"

"Her mother told her she wanted to see the back of her."

"Oh, a family row. Well, perhaps I've never said that to you but I've thought it often enough." She smiled to show she wasn't serious. "I'm sure her mother didn't mean it."

"She's a horrid woman. I'm glad she's not my mother."

"And from all I've heard I'm glad Julia's not my daughter."

Mary said angrily, "That's not fair. You don't know her. There's nothing wrong with her." How could her mother be so mean?

"No," her mother admitted, "I don't know her. Perhaps she's not as bad as she's painted. You'd better tell her to come down and I'll see what she's got to say for herself." But there was no need to call upstairs, for Julia was at the door; Mary wondered how long she'd been there. She had cleaned up and put lipstick on, but she still looked tearful. She had her suitcase in her hand.

"I'll go now, Mrs. Thomson," she said. "I only came to say goodbye to Mary."

"Sit down," Mary's mother said. "You'll have something to eat first. Supper's almost ready. No argument. We'll eat and then we'll see."

The whole family, with Julia, sat down to supper and ate in almost total silence. Even Barbara was quiet, glancing sideways at Julia from time to time, obviously wanting to know what she was doing there but for once too polite to ask. And Bob seemed to find Julia's presence embarrassing, blushing when she looked at him, as she did often. *He's smitten,* Mary thought, *but he's got a girlfriend already.* Bob seemed to remember that, for when they had finished supper he got up hurriedly and went out and they heard the sound of his motorbike as he rode away.

"You and Julia clear away and wash the dishes, Mary, while I have a word with your father," Mrs. Thomson said.

Julia was more cheerful now, even seemed to enjoy wiping dishes as a novelty. "Haven't you a dishwasher?" she asked. Mary ignored her.

"I like it here," Julia said. "They're nice, your family."

"They're all right," said Mary. "Usually."

After they put the dishes away, they went into the living room together and found Mary's mother alone. Julia picked up her case and said, "I'd better go."

"Where?" Mary's mother asked.

Julia didn't answer.

"We'll make up a bed for you in Mary's room. It'll be a tight squeeze, but we'll manage."

Julia opened her mouth to refuse the offer but Mary's

95

mother wouldn't listen. "It's no use arguing. I won't have you wandering the streets in the dark — unless you plan to go back home?"

"No!" Julia said defiantly.

"Then you'll stay here tonight and we'll talk about it tomorrow. And that's that." Mary knew there was no point in arguing. She took Julia's case and, with her friend following, went upstairs.

There was a knock at the bedroom door, and Mary heard her father say, "Can I come in?"

"Yes," said Mary.

"It's time you two stopped talking. You're keeping Barbara awake."

Barbara giggled. She had been chattering as noisily as Mary and Julia.

"I went round to see your mother and father," Mr. Thomson said. "I knew they'd be worried about you."

"I don't suppose they were bothered," Julia said.

"They thought you might have done something silly. They were glad you'd come here. They don't mind if you stay a day or two with us."

"Oh."

"I said we'd be glad to have your company." He looked round the small room and grinned. "That's if you can put up with your accommodation?"

Julia sat up on her camp bed, the blankets pulled up around her and said, "It's cozy, but I don't want to be any trouble, Mr. Thomson."

"What do you think, Mary?" her father said. "And you, Barbara? Shall we let her go?"

"No," they said together.

"Sleep tight, then, and don't go on gossiping all night. You've got the weekend before you."

Julia sighed with pleasure and snuggled down into her bed. Mary could reach out and touch her if she wanted. The room was too small for three of them but it was cozy, as Julia had said. "Good night," Mary said sleepily. But no one answered.

"Aren't you going to see Mrs. Watkins?" Mary's mother asked and explained to Julia. "Mary has made friends with this Mrs. Watkins and on Saturdays helps her with her shopping."

The girls looked at each other. "I don't think I'll go today," said Mary.

"You can't disappoint her. And she'll be waiting for you. I'm sure Julia won't mind going with you."

"Come on," said Julia.

When they were out of sight of the house Julia stopped to light a cigarette. "It's that rich old woman near the park, isn't it?"

Mary was irritated by her friend's tone. "She's not old, at least not all that old, and she's not rich, in spite of what you said. She's really hard up, you can tell, and I feel sort of responsible for her after what we did. So you can stay away if you want, but I'm going to see her and give her a hand. And," she added defiantly, "I like her."

They walked along in silence until they got to the park. "Well," said Mary, "are you coming with me?"

Julia finished her cigarette and ground the stub into the gravel path with her heel. "She might recognize me."

"She hasn't recognized *me*," said Mary.

"It wouldn't be safe," Julia said. "I don't want to risk it. I'll wait here for you."

Mary shrugged her shoulders and went on her own to see Mrs. Watkins. She helped her collect her groceries and carried them back to the house, but she said she couldn't stay as she had a friend with her and must get back home.

"That girl in the park?" Mrs. Watkins said. "I've seen her before somewhere, but can't think where." She smiled at Mary. "Get along then, but I'll miss our chat. I've found one or two more things about Aunt Gladys that might interest you. But next week sometime?"

"Next week," Mary promised. She would have liked to hear more about Gladys Mayhew, but that would have to wait.

"Well?" said Julia. "Duty done?"

"It isn't just duty," Mary said. "I like doing it. And I know a lot more than I did."

"What about?" Julia sounded disbelieving.

"Her Aunt Gladys."

Julia laughed. "Who wants to know about her Aunt Gladys?"

"I do, and I'll show you why." She hadn't intended to let her see the prison diary or anything else from the casket, but Julia had irritated her. Gladys Mayhew was not the sort of woman to be dismissed like that or pushed aside. She refused to be hidden away.

"So, show me," said Julia.

"When we get home. You'll see."

It was afternoon before Barbara was out of the way. Then Mary got the ebony casket, with its mother-of-pearl

98

inlay, from the top of the wardrobe, and opened it to reveal its contents — photographs, papers, the exercise-book diary, the tie, and the brooches. Julia picked up the brooch with the broad arrow, enameled purple, white, and green. "It's pretty," she said.

"That belonged to Gladys Mayhew."

"There's a meaning to it," said Julia. "It's not just a brooch, not just pretty. What does it mean?"

"I'm not sure yet, but I'll find out." said Mary. She picked up the other brooch, the gold pin set with the rough stone of flint. "I know what this one means, though. There's a letter telling all about it. Gladys was given it for breaking a window."

"Gladys! You talk as if you know her."

I think I do, Mary thought. She was beginning to feel sorry she had mentioned her to Julia, for her friend did not understand the importance of Gladys Mayhew, but she would in time.

Julia picked up the exercise book and turned the pages.

"Give it to me," Mary said firmly.

"Why? I've as much right to it as you. More. I took it, didn't I?"

"That's nothing to be proud of."

"Here, take it. What use is it to me? What is it, anyway?"

Mary held the book to her breast protectively. "It's a diary," she said. "Gladys Mayhew's diary of when she was in prison."

"In prison? What for?"

"I told you, throwing a stone, breaking a window."

"No one's sent to prison for that."

99

"The suffragettes were. At any rate they went to prison instead of paying fines."

"You and your Votes for Women!"

Mary was angered by Julia's remark and opened the diary. "Listen to this," she said, and, as she began to read, she saw Gladys in her small cell, with the eye of a wardress looking in at her through the peep hole. " 'I've been looking out of the window. There are two black cats in the yard. I broke a pane just where my mouth can reach when I stand on my chair so I get a little fresh air. I waved my tie out of a broken pane to a woman at a window. Her husband came and they brought their baby and held it up for me to see . . . Christabel appeared at a window in the houses opposite the prison and waved to us. It's been a most exciting morning. I ate 4 potatoes for dinner, but the suet pudding — A magistrate has been to see me to try me for mutiny. I told him I was not sorry for breaking windows, would do the same again if I got the chance & that I did not intend to comply with any 2nd division rules. He sentenced me to 7 days close confinement and had me taken down by six wardresses to this cell with nothing in it except a block of wood fixed to the wall for a chair & a plank bed & pillow, unbreakable opaque windows and double iron doors. God help me to stick it. I can hear the others singing, thank goodness. They brought in a pint of cocoa & a lump of the usual bread.' "

"What is it?" she heard Julia say somewhere. But Julia was not there. Perhaps she was outside the prison in one of the houses on the other side of the road. Perhaps it had been Julia waving from one of the windows out there, but she could not see her now, for the windows in this new cell shut out views of the outside world.

"Mary!" she heard, and felt Julia's hand on hers. "Are you all right?"

She opened her eyes and saw her friend and her room and the window looking out onto the street and the gardens of the houses. She got up and went to look out to the normal world. Two black kittens were playing in the garden next door, watched by the mother cat. Mr. Meadows was chatting to his wife, who was standing at the garden gate proudly holding their new baby. When they saw Mary at the window they held the baby up to show him to her. She waved and turned back.

Julia was gazing at her in puzzlement. "You didn't seem to be with me."

Mary picked up the diary and read the next sentences to herself. "They brought in a pint of cocoa & a lump of the usual bread. Hunger strike commences. We seem to be buried alive."

"What is it, Mary?" Julia asked.

Mary pointed at the words, unable to speak for distress, knowing what was going to happen to Gladys, perhaps not this time, but another time when she would deny herself the food that was brought.

"Hunger strike commences. We seem to be buried alive."

"Why?" Julia asked. "Why did she do that?" But before Mary could answer the door opened and Mary's mother looked in. "Didn't you hear me call? It's time for tea." She looked at Mary and then at the ebony box and the contents spread on the bed. "Hello, what have you got there?"

Mary couldn't speak, but Julia said quickly, "Mrs. Watkins lent Mary some stuff for her Votes for Women project. That's what it is, isn't it, Mary?"

"Tea time," Mary's mother said. "Come along." She looked again at Mary and her eyes showed concern. "I think you're working too hard. You need some fresh air. After tea you'd better go for a walk. You don't want to be cooped up indoors all day."

Mary felt she wanted some fresh air straight away. Perhaps it was that the bedroom was too small for three, but she felt the walls closing in on her, almost as if she was buried alive. She shuddered.

"That was a near thing," Julia said when they went out after tea. "I thought you were going to tell your mother how you got hold of the casket."

"I wish I had," Mary replied. "I wish I had."

Chapter Nine

Emily Watkins turned uncomfortably in her bed. She still suffered from that fall and wondered if she had done more damage than she was ready to admit. But she knew it wasn't that. Something else was niggling away, nothing to do with her old bones.

That friend of Mary's — she *had* seen her before — and she knew where. She had thought so when she stood at her window looking out for Mary. She had seen them talking together before Mary came over the road and her friend went back into the park. She had seen her that other day.

She had seen the girl light a cigarette. Ah, that was it. But it had been driven from her mind when she went to the door to let Mary in. Now she could not hide it from herself: she had seen the two of them together on that awful day when her house had been entered and her precious casket stolen.

She didn't want to believe it, but there was no denying

it. She sat up in bed, switched on her bedside lamp and picked up her book. But the idea wouldn't go away. She tried to concentrate on the murder mystery she was reading, to follow the clues, but her mind kept shifting to the moment when two girls in brown dashed past her and knocked her to the ground. Two girls in brown; she remembered now, two girls in school uniform.

She refused to believe it. It was not Mary, it couldn't be!

She put her book down, switched off the lamp, and tried to settle to sleep. But it was no use. She saw Mary so clearly, standing at the bottom of the garden looking back, as she lay confused and hurt with her groceries scattered around her. Not Mary!

Other thoughts crowded in, little seeds of distrust, details that had puzzled her before. How had Mary known about Nell? And how had she known Aunt Gladys was involved with the Votes-for-Women campaign? She had wondered about Mary's interest in Aunt Gladys, where it had come from. Now she knew.

She wouldn't let herself believe it. Mary was not that sort of girl. But . . . she switched on the lamp again, got up, and went downstairs to make herself a cup of tea. Murphy lay in his basket, looked up at her, and then let his head fall in sleep.

Murphy liked Mary too, and Murphy was never mistaken. Mary was a decent girl, kind and helpful, not at all the sort of girl to do anything dishonest or to wish to hurt an elderly lady like herself — or anyone else, for that matter.

Yet, she told herself, *she knew about my mother Nell and there was only one way she could have known—from the papers in the casket.*

"I must tell Miss Collins," she said aloud, and Murphy, disturbed, meowed. "Do you think I should, Murphy?" Murphy curled up and went to sleep. "That's what I shall do, Murphy, sleep on it."

She did not sleep very well, for her dreams were filled with images of her aunt, who from time to time seemed to change to the girl Mary. First it was Aunt Gladys who was being manhandled by a large, cruel-featured woman in uniform, and then it was Mary, held down by the same woman while Policewoman Collins kept shouting, "Admit it! Own up!" She woke with a start and said, while sleep was still in her eyes, "I can't do it; I can't give her away."

She couldn't think of losing Mary's friendship. She was fond of the girl, whatever she had done, and she thought Mary was genuinely fond of her. The girl could keep the casket and everything in it; she would rather have Mary's friendship than all those other things. They belonged to the past; Mary was part of her life now. Maybe she was foolish to let Mary get away with doing something wrong, but she couldn't risk hurting the girl and spoiling what there was between them. She wouldn't mention it to her. Mary had done wrong once, but Emily Watkins was sure she was not really a bad girl. Everyone behaved badly at some time; she hadn't always been an angel herself, she thought, remembering escapades from her own youth.

She would say nothing, neither to Policewoman Collins nor to Mary. She would encourage Mary to think of her as a good friend, to be trusted to keep a secret. And Mary's wrongdoing would be a secret she would keep to herself, not revealing her knowledge even to Mary herself.

She went downstairs and put some food out for Murphy. ''I wonder if she'll come to see us today, Murphy,'' she said. Murphy paid no attention, neither to her nor his food.

Chapter Ten

Julia spent Sunday morning "helping" Bob as he tinkered with his motorbike. Mary stood by for a moment, but it was obvious Julia didn't want her there and Bob seemed impatient to get rid of her. So she went upstairs to her room and got the casket down from its hiding place. There was no need to hide it, now that Julia had given a reason for its being there. But Mary dreaded her mother's meeting Mrs. Watkins, as would happen one day, and mentioning it. Before then she would have returned it, slipped it into Mrs. Watkins's house, and put it back in its cupboard. She would do it as soon as she had finished reading the diary. She couldn't part with it before.

There was so much she needed to have explained, and Mrs. Watkins was the person who could do that, but she must be careful about what she asked. Once or twice she had almost given herself away.

She opened the exercise book at the date Thursday, 15th July 1909. The writing was clear and strong. She didn't think it was the kind of writing she would be capable of if she had been on a hunger strike. She wondered how Gladys had managed to keep an exercise book with her. Something was not quite right about that.

The wardresses brought in a little pan of water, towel & bit of soap. How long, oh Lord! How long. I feel so weak. Breakfast has just been put in. They have changed my diet to the vegetarian & so have brought a lump of butter beside the usual. I said I did not want any, God help me. I wonder if those outside are thinking of us. I am a coward. Oh Nell I am glad you are not here. It is hard to bear.

Mary paused to see in her mind the photograph of Nell, the girl with the sad and thoughtful eyes, the girl who became Mrs. Watkins's mother, the girl who never forgot how her sister looked after being forcibly fed. How could Gladys think of herself as a coward? Mary wondered if *she* would ever have courage enough to face imprisonment for anything? The thought made her shudder with horror.

She went to the window and looked down to see Julia putting on a crash helmet and sitting astride the pillion of Bob's bike. It roared away and Mary felt cross that her friend was deserting her. She suddenly felt she needed company. She couldn't help but read Gladys's diary, but every time she did she was reminded of what she had done. And yet, at the same time she felt pride, pride in Gladys Mayhew, in a young woman with courage enough to defy authority and to submit to the most awful experiences for a Cause. It was that Cause she needed to understand, not just Gladys Mayhew, but the reasons that drove her to such self-sacrifice. There was nothing among the papers to help her understand. She would have to find the explanation somewhere else, from Mrs. Watkins maybe.

She heard her mother calling and put the papers back in the casket and went downstairs.

"I think Julia has got over her trouble all right, don't you?" Mary's mother said. "I expect she won't mind going home after dinner. I wonder if her mother would let her come camping with us when we go down to Cornwall?"

When Julia returned from her ride with Bob, face all flushed and eyes sparkling, Mrs. Thomson told her the idea she should go on holiday with them.

"That would be great," Julia said. "I'll ask them tonight when I go home."

Mrs. Thomson looked at her husband and Mary saw him wink and look smug with satisfaction. They had sorted out Julia's problems for the moment. Mary wished her own were as easy to deal with.

Julia met her at the school gates the following morning with the news that her parents said they would be glad to let her go camping with the Thomsons. "My mother seemed to like your father," she said. "But then he's nice, isn't he?"

"What about changing schools?" Mary asked.

"I didn't ask, but I expect they'll forget what they said. They never mean what they say, anyway."

After school, Mary hurried home and then went to see Mrs. Watkins. There were things she needed to know, but she would have to be careful about what she asked.

"I'm so glad you've come, my dear," Mrs. Watkins said. "I've been hunting around for things that might interest you. You did say you were doing work at school on the Votes-for-Women campaign?''

Mary nodded. She remembered thinking she had given herself away when she had mentioned it, but Mrs. Watkins evidently hadn't noticed it.

"Come over here and see what I've found." The table was covered with cuttings from newspapers. "I didn't know I had these. Luckily I'd forgotten them; otherwise I would have put them with the photographs and diary in the missing casket." She didn't look at Mary as she spoke and Mary didn't look at her. "I think my mother collected all these. She was proud of her sister. I expect she hid them from her parents though, because they disapproved of their daughter's being mixed up with Mrs. Pankhurst.''

"Mrs. Pankhurst?''

"The leader of the suffragettes. They were the ones who were willing to break the law to bring about a change." She showed Mary a newspaper photograph of a woman being escorted by a large number of policemen; her arm was gripped by a police sergeant, bulky and black-mustached. The woman, square-faced, with the same determined jaw as Gladys Mayhew, looked ahead proudly as if unconcerned at what was happening to her. "That's Mrs. Pankhurst, the first time she was arrested.''

"What had she done?''

"Tried to present a petition to Parliament. You can see it in her hand.''

Mary saw a roll of paper in the woman's right hand. "Was that *all* she did?''

"She was a thorn in the flesh of the Government. They grew to fear what she and her followers would do next.

110

And they did some wild things later, when they seemed to be getting nowhere with their petitions and their demonstrations.''

''And Gladys?'' Mary went to the mantelpiece and took the photograph down to look at it. ''What did she do to get sent to prison so often?''

''Broke a window of a Government office. That was the first time. Smashed windows in stores in Regent Street in London and then set fire to postboxes. I told you they did some wild things. Others were even wilder. But they were all well-intentioned.''

''Surely if *all* the women had banded together they could have changed things.''

Mrs. Watkins looked at Mary and smiled. ''Authority is authority, my dear, police and prisons. Many women did support them and suffered for it, and there were some who supported the cause of Votes for Women but disapproved of the methods used by Mrs. Pankhurst's followers. And strangely enough, there were some women totally opposed to women being given the vote.''

Mary held Gladys's photo in front of her. Apart from the set of her jaw she was an ordinary-looking young woman. Where could she have found the strength to do as she had done?

''What sort of woman was she really? Was she wild?''

''She was a decent young thing, driven to what she did by her beliefs. I adored her, as did my mother. She was so self-reliant, so serious, and yet such good fun. She went to University to study law and then took lessons in shorthand before getting a job in a solicitor's office. It proved useful to her, that shorthand.

111

"We're being very serious," Mrs. Watkins said, "but you did say you were interested. I don't know why a young girl like you should be so eager to know."

"I have an idea."

"What is that?"

"They're planning to change the name of our school."

"What has that to do with my Aunt Gladys?"

"They're going to call it after some man, Thomas Wilton, and I don't think it's fair."

Mrs. Watkins smiled.

"You think I'm being silly," Mary said.

Mrs. Watkins shook her head. "But I still don't see what it's got to do with Aunt Gladys."

Mary didn't answer straight away. Perhaps her idea *was* silly. "I don't see why they can't call it after a woman," she said. "After all, it was a girls' school to being with."

The old lady's eyes lit with delight. "And you think Aunt Gladys is the woman! How exciting! The Gladys Mayhew School. That would be something!"

"You don't think it's silly then?"

"Not a bit of it, but those fuddy-duddies in the Education Office will take some convincing." She looked closely at Mary. "What gave you the idea? And what made you choose Aunt Gladys?"

Mary couldn't say, dared not say. She was still holding the photo of Gladys Mayhew, looking into her eyes, seeing beyond the black and white image. "What color were her eyes?" she said suddenly, knowing they were brown like hers.

"Guess," Mrs. Watkins said.

"They were brown," Mary stated. "I can see."

Mrs. Watkins gently took the photo from her and put it back on the mantel shelf. "I think we've talked enough about Aunt Gladys," she said. "How is your friend? The girl who waited for you outside?"

Mary wondered why she had asked. "She's fine."

"Is she a special friend?"

For a moment Mary wanted to deny Julia was anything special, but it wouldn't be true. "She's my best friend," she said in the end.

"Yes, I see," said Mrs. Watkins.

"But . . . ," said Mary. "You're my friend, aren't you? You're special. In a different way, but special. You don't mind?"

"No, my love, I'm glad. So very glad."

Chapter Eleven

Mary wanted to tell Miss Taylor that she had had an idea for the school's new name, that she had found the name of a former pupil who had done something memorable. But she needed to know a lot more about Gladys Mayhew and about the cause for which she had worked before she could convince anyone of the justice of her claim.

Miss Taylor seemed pleased with what Mary had done on her project so far. "You've found out far more than I thought you could." She had brought several books to help Mary, but there were still questions that none of the books seemed to answer. What was the meaning of the brooch shaped like a portcullis, for example? Miss Taylor showed her a booklet she had found, with the title *A Roll of Honor of Suffragette Prisoners, 1905–1914*. On the front was a drawing of the brooch. Now Mary had a reason for asking what the brooch symbolized. Miss Taylor didn't know, but thought Mrs. Watkins might.

"That's a proud list of names," Miss Taylor said.

"Anyone called Thomson, Mary?" There was, an Edith Thomson, but Mary didn't think she could be related; otherwise, her father would surely have mentioned it.

"He might not have known about it. His family might have been ashamed that a relative of theirs had been sent to prison," Miss Taylor argued.

"Oh no," Mary said. "They must have been proud." As Mrs. Watkins was proud of her Aunt Gladys. When Mary searched the pages and found the name of Gladys Mayhew she too felt a glow of pride that Gladys belonged there. She was surprised to see the names of some men on the list, not many, but enough to show that men too had been willing to challenge the law for the sake of Women's Rights.

"You can borrow the list and take it home. But be careful with it," Miss Taylor said.

Mary thought that would give her a good excuse to ask Mrs. Watkins about the meaning of the brooch, and, deciding to waste no time about it, she went immediately after school. When she got to Mrs. Watkins's house the questions she had been shaping left her mind. As she reached out to knock on the door, it opened and Mrs. Watkins was on the threshold, face white and drawn, eyes worried. In her arms she carried a blanket-wrapped bundle, her cat Murphy.

"Oh, Mary," she said. "I'm so glad you're here. Murphy's not at all well." Murphy lay listlessly in her arms. Mary stretched a hand out to him and the cat opened his eyes and gave a weak whimper. "Hold him for a moment," Mrs. Watkins said, "while I lock up." Mary took him. There was hardly any weight to him. She spoke soft soothing noises, and Murphy opened his eyes to look at her and whimpered sadly.

"Will you come with me, Mary? I'm taking him to the vet. I hope . . . I'm afraid, though. . . ." She looked at Mary and shook her head despairingly. "Let me take him." Mary gently handed her the cat and together they walked toward the busy High Street where the vet had his surgery.

They had to wait their turn. They didn't speak but sat looking at Murphy. He had opened his eyes and looked at Mrs. Watkins as if asking what was happening. Mary saw a tear glistening on the old lady's cheek and put out a hand to her. They sat holding hands until it was time to go in.

"Ah, Mrs. Watkins." Mr. Dixon, the vet, knew her. "What's wrong? Murphy?" He gently took the burden from Mrs. Watkins and put Murphy on his examination table. Murphy seemed to know he was in good hands, for he lay unprotesting while the vet opened the cat's mouth, put his nose down to it, and smelled his breath, then gently felt Murphy's abdomen.

Mrs. Watkins reached for Mary's hands. She was trembling and Mary held tight, wanting to comfort her, to reassure her.

Murphy moaned and stirred, but he didn't have strength enough to stand.

"Well?" whispered Mrs. Watkins. "Can you do anything? I know he's old, but . . ."

Mr. Dixon, hands still gently stroking Murphy, turned his head. Mary saw his eyes and knew. She wanted to look away but she couldn't. She gripped Mrs. Watkins's hand tightly and heard her say, "I don't want him to suffer."

116

"I'll see he doesn't," Mr. Dixon said. "It will only be a moment. He won't know. Will you stay with him?"

No, please no, Mary said to herself. *I couldn't bear it.*

"Of course," Mrs. Watkins said and went to Murphy and touched him lovingly, as Mr. Dixon carefully inserted the needle that brought Murphy peace.

"That's it," he said. "I'll see to the rest if you like."

Mrs. Watkins didn't answer; she was brushing the tears from her cheeks. Then, "Thank you, yes," she said and reached for Mary's hand again.

They walked slowly back to the house. There was no greeting of a soft meow or the feel of fur rubbing against their legs, merely an empty cat basket and a saucer of water. Mrs. Watkins turned away. "Put the kettle on, there's a good girl," she said and went back to the living room.

"It's silly, isn't it?" she said, when Mary brought her a cup of tea. "Silly to become so fond of a dumb animal." She looked at Mary and her eyes filled with tears. "But he wasn't dumb. I always knew just what he meant. Do you think I'm silly, Mary?"

But Mary couldn't trust herself to speak.

"You're late," Mary's mother said. "I expected you back an hour ago. Is anything the matter?"

Mary shook her head. She didn't want to explain.

"You must have something to eat," her mother said later when Mary sat at the supper table gazing without interest at the cottage pie her mother had prepared. "It's one of your favorites."

"I don't feel like eating," she said, but she couldn't

117

explain. If she mentioned Murphy she would burst into tears and none of them would understand.

"Perhaps you're coming down with something," her mother said. "Get off to bed and I'll bring you a hot-water bottle and something to drink."

Mary was glad to leave them and go to her bedroom. She thought she would be better left by herself to get over her misery, but she couldn't help wondering about Mrs. Watkins, all alone in that big house, without the cat that had kept her company for so long. She had to take her mind off such thoughts.

She opened the diary. That would not be likely to cheer her up, but at least it would stop her thinking about Murphy. She wished now she had had the courage to stroke him while the vet put him to sleep. But she hadn't.

She began to read.

We are practically underground here. The window high in the wall seems to be at ground level. The Chaplain came. He was rather nice. He asked me if I wanted anything. I asked if I could have a library book. He said he was very sorry to see me like this. I could not keep back a few tears when he had gone. I feel so weak . . . I suppose Mother and Father are enjoying the sea air at Bridlington. Thank God they don't know where I am . . . The bang of the double doors is terrible. It seems strange to think of all who we love going about their business in the usual way while we—Oh! I do feel blubbery. I expect it is because I am losing my strength. I should like to have a jolly good cry.

Mary couldn't hold back her tears. It was no use. She could see Aunt Gladys in the cell, but she could see Mrs.

Watkins so much more clearly, standing at her front door holding Murphy in her arms. She began to sob at the recollection.

"What is it, my love?" she heard her mother say and saw her bending over her. "My goodness, you are hot. I think you have a fever." She went to the bedroom door and called downstairs. "Bill, come and have a look at Mary. I think she's really ill."

Mary's father came and she saw him looking down at her. *He's rather nice,* she thought.

"Can I get anything for you?" he asked.

She thought there were a lot of things but she only said, "A library book."

He disappeared, and she wondered what he had done with himself to vanish so completely. There was a muttering going on outside the cell — no, not the cell, wherever she was. Someone peered at her through the peep hole.

"We'd better get the doctor to have a look at her if she's no better in the morning." She heard that quite clearly and wondered what a doctor could do to help. All anyone could do to help was to release her. That was all. Release her. She began to wish she had gone to Bridlington with her parents and Nell. "Nell!" she called out.

Her mother appeared at the door and came over to her. "What is it, Mary?"

"I'm all right, Mum," she said. "I was dreaming." But if it was a dream it was much more real than usual, and the fragments of it were still haunting her so that when she closed her eyes to try to sleep she saw bare walls again, a window set high with thick glass letting only gray light through. She opened her eyes and saw instead her own room, Barbara's bed, untidy as usual, on the other side, and the window with the late evening sun shining through onto the wardrobe with the casket on top. The tie, with its colors of purple, white, and green, was hanging from it. She tried to sit up to get it, but her mother stopped her.

"What do you want?" she said.

"The tie there," Mary said.

Her mother passed it to Mary and she held it a moment and then put it under her pillow and closed her eyes. It was comforting to have it so close. She slept.

"You must have something to eat, darling," Mary heard her mother saying. "I've brought you an egg, done just as you like it."

Mary sat up and pulled the tray toward her, but she couldn't face food. She looked apologetically at her mother. "I'm sorry, Mum. I don't fancy anything."

"Have some bread. It's sliced really thinly. You can manage that."

Mary reached her hand out for it, but the thought of eating anything made her heave with sickness.

"Ah well," her mother said, resigned. "We've asked the doctor to call, so we'll soon know the worst. Did something happen yesterday? You came in after school looking so upset."

Mary remembered and began to feel tearful, but it wasn't the thought of Murphy that was upsetting her now; it was more serious even than that.

"Can I get you anything? Something to read maybe after you've had a wash. Can you get up?"

She felt too weak to go to the bathroom, so her mother brought a bowl of water, some soap, and her toothbrush. She felt a little better afterward but still couldn't face any breakfast. Her mind was clearer this morning, but she remembered the strange feeling she had had the night before. She had seen the cell so clearly where Gladys Mayhew had begun her hunger strike. Now all she could see was her own bedroom, cozy and familiar with all her own things about her. She saw the exercise book — Gladys's prison diary — on the bookshelves beside her bed. She wasn't sure she was in the mood to share more of Gladys Mayhew's experiences, yet she needed to know how she had faced up to her hunger strike. Had she given way in the end? Had her will been strong enough to hold out?

She was about to pick up the diary when she heard the front doorbell, a man's voice, and footsteps on the stairs. "The doctor, dear," her mother said and began to explain Mary's fever to him.

"Well, young lady," he said. "What have you been up to?"

Nothing, she wanted to say, but no sooner had she opened her mouth to speak than he thrust a thermometer under her tongue and felt her pulse.

"Hm," he said after a while. "Hm." Mary's mother looked anxiously at him. "She's got a few years left in her yet," he said and laughed. He seemed to find Mary's illness amusing. "Bowels all right?" he asked.

"I think so," said Mrs. Thomson. She looked enquiringly at her daughter.

"Yes," Mary said.

"Eating?" said the doctor.

121

"Not very well. She usually has such a hearty appetite, but she couldn't face supper or breakfast."

"Have to do something about that. Can't have you wasting away. Get something down you, young woman. You can manage something if you try. No patience with that sort of thing."

"What sort of thing?" Mary's mother asked sharply. "Are you suggesting there's nothing wrong with her? That she's putting it on?"

"No, not at all," the doctor protested. "Can't always tell. Some viral infection. There's a lot of it about. But you must encourage her to eat. Eh, young lady?" He smiled cheerfully down at her and took out a prescription pad and wrote. "Tablets three times a day. May not do her much good, but can't do her much harm either." He breezed off and Mary heard his voice reverberating down the stairs. *Thank you*, she said to herself and picked up the diary to read.

I slept well but was aroused by someone ringing the bell. The Doctor was sent for. I am getting weaker, I've applied for the Chaplain. The wardress told me to get my clothes on as they were going to take my bed out . . . Part of the process seems to be to degrade us by not allowing us to wash properly. Last night I had only my drinking can of water to wash in. I asked the wardress if you were not supposed to wash at night & she said "In this part of the prison you are only supposed to wash in the morning." They understand refined torture in Holloway . . . I do not like the Governor and should not trust him. I wish I could faint or something of that sort. How long I wonder can I

live without food & without air . . . The Doctor has been.
He seems much amused & tried to persuade me to desist.
A nice fat old wardress who I take to be the Matron of the
Hospital & who can smile always comes with him which
is a comfort . . . 54 hours without food. God help me to
hold out. I feel so chokey when I think of the outside
world.''

She stopped reading and instead began to think of Mrs.
Watkins. She wished she could get up and go to her, but
it was all she could do to get as far as the bathroom.

"Is that you?" she heard her mother call.

Who else could it be, she thought, *a ghost*? And there did
seem to be ghosts inhabiting her mind if not her room,
Gladys Mayhew and Nell, and the Governor who looked
like Mr. Wardle, the Headmaster, and the fat wardress
who had a smile like her mother's.

Her mother arrived to help her back to bed. "Is there
anything I can do for you?" she said. *Yes*, thought Mary,
I'd like you to go and see that Mrs. Watkins is all right, but
she didn't dare let the two of them meet now her mother
knew about the casket.

"I've sent a message to school," her mother said.
"Told them you'd go back as soon as you were better."

I hope that won't be long, Mary thought. *I hate it here.*
But in a way she was enjoying herself. She wasn't often ill
and there was something comforting in having her mother
fuss about her, tuck the bedclothes round her, bring her
tempting things to eat, even if she couldn't touch them.

"I wish . . . ," she began.

"What?" her mother said.

123

But she couldn't tell her. She wished she knew how Mrs. Watkins was, what she had done with the cat basket, and the unused tins of cat food they had bought last Saturday. It would be horrid to be reminded all the time of Murphy. Poor Murphy. Poor Mrs. Watkins.

Chapter Twelve

Mary knew her mother was worried about her not eating, but she could do nothing about it. Whatever her mother brought to tempt her, it still made her feel ill to think of food. She tried to take some thin bread and butter, but her throat was sore and she was unable to swallow.

The doctor came to see her, but this time it was a younger one who, though he was more sympathetic than the first, could still do nothing to make her better. He could see no reason why she shouldn't be eating, he said, and when he left the room to talk to Mary's mother, Mary could hear them on the landing, voices low and concerned.

"We'll just have to hope it'll take its course," the doctor said. "But it seems to me there's something behind her sickness. Do you know of any reason why she should be anxious about anything?" Mary couldn't hear her mother's reply for they moved downstairs, and she heard the front door close as the doctor left.

Mary reached down for the diary. Her mother had put

the casket beside the bed so that she didn't need to climb up to the wardrobe for it. When she had done that yesterday she had fallen and alarmed her mother. Now she could touch the tie, look at the brooches, and read the diary whenever she wanted.

She couldn't read for long. It upset her to think of Gladys in her dark and tiny cell, getting weaker and weaker with every hour she refused food. And thinking of Gladys made her think of Mrs. Watkins, and that worried her even more. She felt like weeping whenever she thought of the old lady in her lonely house. *Please forgive me*, she said to Mrs. Watkins in her mind. All the excuses she had made up for not returning the casket no longer seemed reasonable. She should have gone straight back that very first day and admitted what she had done.

She opened the diary at the last words she had read. "I feel so chokey when I think of the outside world." Then Saturday, 17th July. "The Doctor has been & tried to persuade me to give up the Hunger Strike by saying I was not so robust as the others. What would my Mother say and so on."

What would *her* mother say if she knew what she had done? What would Miss Taylor say and everyone at school? It was no use telling herself it was Julia's fault. That didn't excuse what she had done.

Her mother came in. "I've brought you some chicken soup, love. I'm sure you could manage a little." She smiled, but Mary saw anxiety in her eyes.

"I'm sorry," Mary said, near tears. She wished she could explain, but what could she say?

"I'll leave it here anyway. Try to have a sip. We want you fit for the holidays."

The holidays. Mary sighed and tried to take her mind to the beach at Perranporth, in Cornwall, her favorite place in the whole world. For a moment she saw the miles-long stretch of sand and the surf-capped breakers rolling in from the sea, but her imagination couldn't hold the picture for more than an instant before an image of Gladys Mayhew lying stretched out on her hard prison bed blotted it out.

She woke with a start. She had fallen asleep and thought she had heard the clang of a prison door, but it was the sound of a van door in the street outside being slammed shut. Ordinary everyday sounds would never seem the same again.

She reached down into the casket to pick up the diary, but her fingers touched something that had been caught under the satin lining of the box. She made an effort and drew it out. It was an envelope; she opened it and took hold of the sheets of paper in it but was too exhausted to do more. She lay with the paper in her hands and in a strange dreamy state wondered where she was. She knew she had fallen asleep again. A bird outside her window had wakened her.

She felt the papers in her hand and remembered. She half sat up to read and saw firm, carefully formed handwriting, of the sort called copper-plate, written by someone in authority, she thought, for the downstrokes were thick and dominant.

"My dear daughter," the letter began.

I cannot think you have forgotten the obligation you owe

to your mother and myself but your conduct seems to suggest that. Can you imagine the distress your mother is caused every time she reads in the papers of your latest folly? I have tried to understand what it is that makes you behave so, but it is beyond me.

The law, however unjust it may seem to you, is still the law. A civilised people, such as the English are, has learnt to accept that. There is a process by which the law can be changed and that process — the will of parliament — is the only way. Your challenge to the Government by your wilful and criminal behaviour unfits you for any share in political decisions. You and the followers of Mrs. Pankhurst, by your shameless disregard for the law, have disqualified yourselves from any right to share in the process of change.

What does your mother want with a vote? When I use my vote I consider her needs as much as I do my own. Why should not this be sufficient for you?

But I know it is hopeless to reason with you. You were always a stubborn child, determined to get your own way, come what may. Well, you must take your punishment, one you richly deserve.

I have forbidden your sister to have any communication with you. I hope you will respect my wishes in this and not make life more difficult for her than it already is by her being your sister.

In spite of everything you have done to bring disgrace upon us, your mother and I are prepared to forgive you and receive you once again into the bosom of our family if you will undertake to have nothing more to do with such follies as the campaign for women's votes.

I hope you may yet see reason, Your Father, Charles Mayhew.

The signature was written with a flourish.

Mary lay back, exhausted. What a horrid man! She could see him. She had seen him in the snapshot on Bridlington beach. She could never have imagined from his picture that he could be so — she tried to find a word to describe her feelings about him — so smug and pompous and unforgiving. She wondered how Gladys had felt when she received the letter and what had made her keep it. She would have torn it up if it had come from her father. But then her father would never have behaved like that.

No? What if her father knew about her stealing the casket — what would her father think of that? He might not be pompous, but he might well be unforgiving and she couldn't bear the thought of his knowing.

She turned her face to the pillow to try to stop her weeping, but it was no use. She couldn't help herself.

She slept, waking from time to time, aware of her mother or her father coming in to look at her. Once they came in to move Barbara's bed out of the room. *No,* she wanted to say, *don't do that, I want my sister here with me.*

She thought her mother stayed with her a long time, for she woke often during the night to see her sitting beside the bed. Once her mother passed her a glass of water and she drank it and felt a little better. Then it was her father sitting there, and she lay watching him, his head nodding before he jolted himself awake and looked anxiously at her, smiling when he saw her eyes were open.

''What is it?'' he said.

She shook her head and closed her eyes. He mustn't know.

It was several days before she felt strong enough to read the diary again.

Sunday, 18th July. I had a fairly good night but dreaming of food all the time. I find it was Sat. yesterday & not Friday as I thought. The Governor came early. I said I had nothing to say. He said he was very sorry. I feel more cheerful today. I've had quite long talks with Mary Allen through the wall. Dinner time today will be 96 hours without food. The younger Doctor has been. He felt my pulse for ever so long both sitting up and lying down. I wonder if I shall be sent to Hospital.''

Mary looked up to see her mother at the door. "They won't send me to the hospital, will they?" she said.

Her mother shook her head. "No. I can look after you, my love. But you must try to eat. That's the main thing now the fever has gone. I've got some beef tea for you. That's what my grandmother used to give us, that and calves-foot jelly, whenever we were poorly."

"I don't like the sound of that," Mary said.

"But you'll like the beef tea, I'm sure."

She was able to take a few sips without trouble and her mother was pleased. "That's a start," she said. She picked up the diary. "This seems to have caught your interest. You've had your nose in it whenever you've been awake." Mary wanted to snatch it away, but hadn't the strength. Her mother read a passage. "My feet are like stones," she read and then said, "Are you warm enough, Mary? Are you sure? I'll get you a hot-water bottle."

130

"I'm all right, Mum." She held her hand out for the diary and her mother let her have it. Mary read silently on: "I shall have a tale to tell if I get out alive. I suppose everyone is going to Church now. I hope they'll remember we poor wretches. 'To Freedom's Cause till death!' My feet are warmer now."

"You've a visitor," her mother said. "I've warned her you may get tired, so she mustn't stay long, but I'm sure you'll be glad to see her."

Julia appeared from behind Mary's mother. She carried a large basket of fruit and put it down close to Mary's bed. "It's from the class. We wanted to cheer you up. Everyone gave something, even Miss Robinson when she heard about it. She sent a special message, telling you not to worry about work. You'll soon catch up, she says."

Julia sat beside the bed and looked hard at Mary. "You do look awful," she said after a while.

"Thank you very much," said Mary.

"Well, you do, but I expect you'll get over it. I don't know why it's taking you so long."

Mary looked at the grapes, bananas, and cherries, but could rouse no interest in them. "You don't know anything about Mrs. Watkins, do you?" she asked.

"That old biddy! Why should I know anything about her?"

Mary was beginning to feel tired and more so when Julia talked like that. She felt cross with her friend but hadn't the energy to show it. She lay still for a while and watched Julia choose a bright red cherry from the basket of fruit and eat it, smacking her lips with pleasure.

"Will you go and see her?"

"Me! Not likely!"

"Please."

"Why?"

"I'm worried about her." She paused. Julia selected another cherry and popped it into her mouth. "She's on her own and no one ever goes to visit her. I wish . . ."

"Oh, all right. But you'll be to blame if she recognizes me."

"She won't. She's already seen you anyway and didn't say anything."

Julia took another cherry and said, "They're good. You'd better have one before I finish them."

But Mary was only interested in Mrs. Watkins. "Promise you'll go and see her."

"I promise," said Julia.

"Take her some of this," Mary said, pointing to the fruit.

"It's for you." Julia was indignant. "We collected for you, not Mrs. Watkins."

"Take it, please. Tell her it's from school."

Julia shook her head as if she couldn't understand her friend, but she did as Mary asked and took some fruit out of the basket. "Is that enough?" Mary nodded. "I'll take it now then," Julia said, "or I'll be tempted to eat it myself."

"Give her my love," Mary said. "Tell her I'll see her when I'm better."

When Julia had gone Mary looked at the fruit, but wasn't tempted to eat. Perhaps tomorrow, she told herself.

*

132

The next day she was able to eat a little breakfast and felt well enough to get up for a short time, but she quickly became exhausted. She hoped Julia had kept her promise to go to see Mrs. Watkins, for she felt responsible for her — and guilty. She tried not to think of that but whenever she touched the tie or one of the brooches she was reminded and she couldn't help going on with the diary.

Monday, 19th July.

I had rather a bad night. I was sure my bed was stuffed with stones. My poor bones ached terribly. When the Doctor came I asked if he could not send me to Hospital. He said as a matter of fact he was going to send me there but I must take some nourishment. At a little after 12 o'clock just after dinner had been thrust in, the Hospital Matron & 2 prisoners with a carrying chair came for me and carried me to the Hospital. They put me to bed & gave me a hot water bottle and brought me jelly, milk, bread & butter etc. which of course I refused. The Doctor came & talked & talked but I said I would not budge. Then he came and asked me where I wanted what was left of me to be sent at the end of the month. I said I did not think there would be any to send anywhere.

She could read no more, couldn't bear to imagine the agony that Gladys was suffering, and when her mother brought in a tray with a milk, jelly, and some thin bread and butter, she couldn't believe it. She burst into tears and buried her head in the pillow. "No! No!" she cried. "No!"

She felt her mother's arms about her shoulders. "I didn't mean it," she said. "I didn't want to take it. I'm not wicked. Please." She couldn't stop weeping but didn't know why.

"There, there," she heard her mother say. "Of course you didn't. Whatever it was. I know you, my love. You're not wicked, believe me."

But she was, whatever her mother said. She wished she could confide in her and began to speak, but her mother said, "Just have a little. You'll feel better when you've had something. It'll slip down without any trouble, you'll see." She held a spoonful of jelly up to Mary's mouth and it did slip down easily. Mary took the spoon from her mother and ate, slowly at first and then almost greedily. She hadn't realized how hungry she was.

"Better for that?" her mother said. She nodded. "Then dry your eyes and go to sleep. You look worn out."

She couldn't sleep. And, though she was almost at the end of the diary, with only two or three pages left, she couldn't bear to read it now. She put it back in the casket, with the rest of the things and pushed it out of sight under the bed, as if in that way she could push it out of her mind. But it was there all the time, to remind her of that moment of weakness and folly when she had run off with Mrs. Watkins's treasures in her arms.

Chapter Thirteen

Mary slowly improved, but she still felt listless. The young doctor came again and said she had recovered from the infection and all she needed now was plenty of good food and fresh air. He said he didn't know why she wasn't already back to normal.

"But young women are a puzzle," he said. "I'll never understand them." He smiled cheerfully.

"He's nice, isn't he?" her mother said when she had seen the doctor out.

"I suppose he's all right," Mary said. She knew he couldn't have done anything to set her mind at rest.

"You can get up soon and come downstairs if you feel like it."

But Mary didn't feel like it and lay in bed staring at the ceiling, wondering about Mrs. Watkins and Gladys Mayhew. Once she reached under the bed intending to get the diary out, but touching the casket brought that horrid feeling of guilt back to her. *I wish I'd had nothing to do with it*, she thought. *I wish I'd never seen it.* But it was there, and there was no wishing it away. She got up and looked on her bookshelves for something to read, something to take her mind off her troubles. She was still searching when she heard her mother call up, in a voice that held surprise and delight, "There's a visitor for you, Mary."

Mary got back into bed and pulled the blanket round her. She didn't want any visitors, not now, unless it was Julia to bring her news of Mrs. Watkins. She heard her mother open the door but pretended to sleep, with her face to the wall so that she wouldn't be disturbed.

"Oh, I'm sorry," she heard her mother whisper. "I'm afraid she's asleep."

"Don't wake her. I'll come back some other time." It was a voice she knew. She turned her head, sat up, and said, "Don't go, Mrs. Watkins. Don't go."

Her mother left them alone, and Mrs. Watkins sat beside the bed and took hold of Mary's hand. "Well, you seem to have given everybody quite a fright. I was beginning to think you'd forgotten all about me. And then your friend came to see me and told me you were in bed."

"My friend."

"Julia." Mrs. Watkins smiled. "We got on very well after a while. She's a headstrong young thing, isn't she? I can see she'd have been in plenty of trouble if she'd known my Aunt Gladys. She'd have been one of the wildest of those young women, I bet." She looked at Mary with concern. "Don't let me tire you. Tell me if you want me to go. I shan't be hurt."

Mary shook her head but said nothing.

"We had a long talk, your friend and I. And I lent her quite a lot of old photographs for her work on fashion. I'm sure she'll put them to good use."

She knows, thought Mary. There had been something in the way she'd spoken of Julia. She dropped her head, unwilling to look Mrs. Watkins in the eye.

"Have you anything to tell me, Mary?"

"You know, don't you?"

"Yes, I know."

"Did Julia tell you?"

"She didn't need to, but she told me."

"How long . . . How long have you known?"

"I think I knew from the start, but I didn't want to believe it."

"I'm sorry," Mary said and burst into tears. "I hate myself," she said between sobs. She felt a hand take hold of her chin and lift her head up. She opened her eyes and saw Mrs. Watkins smiling at her.

"We can all do silly things, my dear — me, your friend Julia, my Aunt Gladys."

"She wasn't silly. She believed in something. She . . ." Mary couldn't say what she felt about Gladys. She wasn't sure she understood why Gladys had behaved as she had, but there was something very special about her.

"You learned that?"

Mary nodded.

"From the diary?"

Guilt again swept over Mary and, looking away, she said, "I'm sorry I stole your memories."

Mrs. Watkins laughed. "You couldn't steal those, my dear. You brought them to life again by your interest in my aunt."

"It's under the bed."

"I'm too stiff to crawl down there," Mrs Watkins said,

and Mary got out of bed, knelt down, and brought the casket out. She handed it to Mrs. Watkins, got back into bed, and said, ''I wanted to do this before, straight away, every day, but didn't dare.''

Mrs. Watkins leaned over and kissed her on the cheek, held the casket on her lap, and stared silently at it for a while.

''I can never read the diary,'' she said. ''I find it too upsetting. Have you read it through?''

''Not quite all. I couldn't finish it. It didn't seem right, somehow.''

''I think Aunt Gladys would be pleased to think a girl like you was reading it. Perhaps that was why she wrote it, so that the sort of thing she endured should not be forgotten, that the things she believed in should be cherished.'' She opened the casket and took out the exercise book and held it for a moment.

''There were three sheets of toilet paper.''

''They're still there,'' said Mary, and opened the exercise book to show them.

''I expect you wondered what they were doing in a collection like this. You don't think the prison authorities would have let her keep a diary if they'd known? She used to tell me how she saved up sheets of toilet paper each time she went to the lavatory. She wrote her diary on those, in shorthand, and hid them in her clothing. She smuggled them out and copied it up later in that old book there.'' She chuckled. ''It's funny to think of history being written on toilet paper, isn't it?'' Mary giggled, and then they began laughing together so heartily that Mary's mother came to find out what the joke was.

Mrs. Watkins rubbed tears of laughter from her eyes. "A private joke," she said and began laughing again.

"You're doing our Mary a world of good," Mrs. Thomson said.

"And she's doing the same for me," said Mrs. Watkins.

"I'll go and get us all a drink," Mary's mother said.

"Where have you got to in the diary?" Mrs. Watkins asked.

"Almost the last page."

"Then read it to me."

Mary opened the diary and began to read. " 'The other Doctor came. I had a foot bath & then the wardress who was very nice settled me for the night. At 6.20 the Governor came with the Matron & said "Are you feeling miserable?" I said "Not at all I'm very comfortable." He said "Are you still obstinate?" "Yes." "Well I have some news for you. You are to be released." He told me to be very quiet & move about slowly & he would send a wardress to dress me & to bring me some brandy in a beaten egg. As soon as he had gone I got up & waited & at about 7.20 after the Matron had brought my bag a wardress came for me & I was taken in a cab to a friend's house. Christabel came just as I was put to bed. I never was so happy in my life!' "

Mary looked at Mrs. Watkins and saw that tears, not of laughter now, but of pride in her aunt, were flowing freely down her cheeks. Mary wanted to ask her so much, but now was not the time. That would come later.

There was a rattle of cups at the door, and Mary's mother appeared with coffee for Mrs. Watkins and herself and a glass of hot milk for Mary. When Mrs. Thomson saw the

139

casket she said, "It was so good of you to let Mary borrow all that."

Smiling at Mary, Mrs. Watkins said, "I knew she'd take good care of it. My Aunt Gladys would approve of her."

"Aunt Gladys?"

"Mary will tell you all about her, I expect." Mary's mother looked into the casket and saw the enameled brooch. "That's interesting," she said. "What is it? It's no ordinary brooch." She reached her hand into the casket and then turned to Mrs. Watkins. "May I?"

"Yes. Have a good look at it. It belonged to my aunt. All these things belonged to her. The brooch was a gift from Mrs. Pankhurst. It was designed by her daughter Sylvia and represents the prison gate. The Holloway Brooch, they called it. All the women who went to prison for their belief in Women's Suffrage were given one."

"A badge of honor, then," said Mary's mother.

"A Badge of Honor," repeated Mrs. Watkins.

Chapter Fourteen

Soon Mary was well enough to go back to school, but she had to go to see Mrs. Watkins first, to return the casket to her. Mrs. Watkins had left it with her so that she could make notes of anything she wanted for school, but Mary wanted her to have it back, and all her precious memories of her Aunt Gladys.

She had not been to the house since Murphy died. She would miss his welcoming rub against her legs. She wondered if Mrs. Watkins might like one of the black kittens from next door. Mrs. Meadows wanted to find good homes for them.

Mrs. Watkins opened the door to her. "It's so good to see you on your feet again. I've missed your visits. And I've got a surprise for you." She led the way into the kitchen. "There," she said.

A black kitten was lapping at a bowl of milk. "Your neighbor brought it round last night. I'd told your mother how I missed Murphy. It's not the same," she added sadly, "but she's a sweet wee thing." She picked the kitten up and took it with her into the living room. Mary followed and put the casket on the table.

"I'm sorry," she said.

"Don't say any more about it. I lent it to you, don't you remember?" She sat with the kitten on her lap, stroking it. "Have you had any more thoughts about that idea of yours?"

Mary looked puzzled.

"That idea about the Gladys Mayhew School." Mrs. Watkins took the portcullis badge out of the casket and looked at it. Mary could see she was glad to have it back. "Wouldn't Gladys have been proud at the thought?"

"I don't suppose anyone will agree with me. Nobody else knows anything about her."

"Then tell them. You can do it. If you believe in it strongly enough yourself."

"I wouldn't know where to begin."

"Let's work it out. Try the case on me."

Mary could see Mrs. Watkins had her aunt's persistent determination. She was not going to let the idea vanish into thin air.

"It was only a vague notion," Mary said.

"But a good one. Who's ever heard of Thomas Wilton, anyway? Why shouldn't the school be named after a woman?"

They began considering the arguments, and before long Mary had found all sorts of reasons why Gladys Mayhew should be remembered.

"I've tired you out," Mrs. Watkins said after they had

talked and argued for forty minutes or so. Mary did feel tired, but she was grateful for having had her thoughts sharpened. Now she felt she could persuade anyone, even Joe Simpson, of the need to do justice to the memory of Gladys Mayhew.

When she mentioned her idea to Miss Taylor she began to have second thoughts, but Miss Taylor was enthusiastic. "You've found someone — a rival to Thomas Wilton, a woman. Good. So let's see what we can do now. You'd better try your notion on the class first. And then put it to the Headmaster and the school governors."

"I couldn't do that."

"Why not?"

"Couldn't you do it for me?"

Miss Taylor shook her head. "No. It's your idea. Your responsibility."

It *was* her idea. Hers and Mrs. Watkins's. She would go on with it, even if the thought of presenting it to the school governors was a daunting prospect. She could do it. She would do it.

She gave the arguments to the class, read passages from the diary to them, and told them of the courage with which Gladys Mayhew met her prison sentences. And she explained why Gladys and women like her had felt driven to make their protests in order to win the vote. She was surprised at how readily they agreed with her proposal about the name of the school. After the class, as she was walking out of school with Julia, Joe Simpson caught up with them.

"You weren't making all that up?" he said.

"Of course not," Mary said indignantly.

"She was quite a one, that Gladys, wasn't she? I reckon she earned the right to vote." He ran off, whistling shrilly, to catch up with his friends.

"I don't believe it!" said Julia.

Miss Robinson sent for Mary the next day. "Miss Taylor and I have persuaded Mr. Wardle that you should appear before the school governors when they meet tomorrow."

"Tomorrow?" Mary gulped. She couldn't. She needed time.

Miss Robinson went on, "Nothing will come of it, unfortunately. They're too set in their ways. They won't take kindly to the fact that a girl from this school broke the law, however far back in the past it was and whatever her reasons. But it will do them good to have something different to think about, to see that our present girls have minds and ideas of their own." She waited for Mary to say something, but she couldn't find words to express her dismay at the thought of presenting her case — or the case of Gladys Mayhew — to a gathering of strangers.

"Well?" Miss Robinson said. "Are you ready for them?"

As ready as I'll ever be, she thought, but for a moment she wished she had never had such a mad idea.

She hurried from school to see Mrs. Watkins to tell her how quickly the matter was to be put to the test. "I wish you could be there with me," she said.

"Gladys Mayhew will be with you, in spirit," Mrs. Watkins assured her. "You won't let her down, I know."

144

She took the photograph of Gladys from the mantel shelf and handed it to Mary. "Take that with you to give you heart, and take this too." She put the portcullis badge into Mary's hands. "Tell them what it meant. Tell them what it means, that's the important thing."

That night Mary found it difficult to get to sleep. She found herself looking again and again at the photo of Gladys Mayhew, trying to get some inspiration from her. But the result of tomorrow's meeting depended on her, Mary Thomson, not on Gladys Mayhew.

The next day was one of misery and nervousness until, halfway through the afternoon, a message came for her to present herself at the Head's office in readiness to meet the school governors. She wished — but it was no use wishing Mrs. Watkins could be with her — she was on her own. It was up to her.

"Well, young woman," the large man at the other end of the table greeted her when she was summoned into the meeting. "Make yourself at ease." Twenty-four eyes turned to her, twelve grim faces, pretending to be interested in what she had to say, expecting her to make a fool of herself, she was sure. She saw Mr. Wardle nodding encouragingly and then he said, "I've told the governors of your feeling that we should consider calling the school after one of its girls."

Mary swallowed. She had known just what she was going to say but, looking around the table at the seven men and five women waiting for her to speak, her mind went blank.

"What's that you have in your hand?" the woman nearest to her said. Mary had forgotten she was holding the badge and the photo Mrs. Watkins had lent her. She glanced down and saw the firm chin, the clear eyes, the steady look of Gladys Mayhew; courage returned.

"The photo of a woman who went to this school and who I think deserves to be remembered." She passed it to the woman who looked intently at it and then gave it to her neighbor. It went round the table.

"And this," said Mary, holding up the badge so that all could see it, "this is a badge she won for her courage."

"Her courage? In what? One of the wars?" The chairman said.

"Yes," said Mary, suddenly bringing to mind all she wanted to say. "But not the sort of war you're thinking of. It was like a war, a battle to win women the right to have a say in how the country was governed. She — Gladys Mayhew" — she pointed to the photograph now standing on the table in front of the members — "that's Gladys Mayhew. She was a suffragette. She believed women deserved the vote as much as men, and when the government of the day refused to listen and would not even let women ask questions at public meetings, she joined others in marching and demonstrating for that right. She broke windows in protest and went to prison to draw attention to the cause."

"She went to prison!" exclaimed a woman, who was wearing a florid, wide-brimmed hat and was sitting next to the chairman.

"Three times," said Mary calmly, much more calmly than she felt. She could sense hostility.

"One of those!" said the woman.

"So was my grandmother," said a thin bespectacled man to Mary's right. He smiled at Mary, put out his hand to the photo, looked hard at it, and said, "She looks a very ordinary young woman."

"She was until she took up the cause, I think," said Mary.

"You know a lot about her?" the thin man said.

"I've found out quite a lot. Her name is on the old Honors Board," she said. "For winning a scholarship to the university."

"Ah, that's better," said the chairman. "That's the sort of thing we want to encourage."

"But hardly breaking the law," said the woman in the hat. "We don't want our girls to look up to anyone doing that sort of thing."

"She was a fine woman," said the thin man.

"Did *you* know this Gladys Mayhew?" the chairman said.

"No. I mean my grandmother. A woman of principle. A strict churchgoer, a most responsible woman as I remember, but she got into trouble with the law too, for what she believed in."

"There's no excuse for that sort of thing," said the hat.

The thin man looked over his glasses at her. "You owe a great deal to those women," he said. "We all owe a great deal to them." He looked at Mary. "Go on. Tell us more."

"Gladys Mayhew went on a hunger strike when she was in prison. I've seen the diary she kept in her cell." She heard a snort of disapproval from the hat. "Whatever else she was," Mary exclaimed angrily, "she was brave, she believed in something and did not hesitate to do what she

147

thought was right. I think she's someone worth thinking about, someone who deserves to be honored by her old school. I think she brought honor to the school by what she did." She was aware that Mr. Wardle was pursing his lips and was making little movements with his fingers as a signal to her to be careful. But she did not mind what she said. "I would be proud to go to the Gladys Mayhew School, but . . ." She stopped herself just in time. She was going to say "What is there to be proud of about Thomas Wilton?"

The thin man smiled and she saw that the eyes of the other men and women round the table were not unfriendly. One or two nodded as if they liked what they saw. But the woman in the hat was not to be appeased. "I sometimes wonder what they teach in schools nowadays. In my day . . ."

"Yes," the chairman interrupted. "We have a decision to make. Thank you, Mary. We're very glad you came."

Mary looked over to Mr. Wardle. Was that all? Weren't they going to tell her what they thought? The Headmaster echoed what the chairman had said. "Thank you very much, Mary. You can go back to your class now."

But classes had ended for the day, the corridors and classrooms were empty, and Mary felt empty too and disappointed. She had not said half of what she meant to say. They hadn't given her the chance. They would know all there was to know about Thomas Wilton; she had hardly told them anything about Gladys Mayhew.

"Well? How did it go?" She turned to see Miss Taylor following her out of school.

"I don't know. I made a mess of things."

"What did they decide?"

148

"I don't know. After they'd heard me making a fool of myself they told me to go." She looked at the notice board at the school gates. "There we are. The Thomas Wilton School. That's what it will be next term."

"You did your best. And anyway you never know. You may have convinced them."

Mary turned away disconsolately.

"Aren't you going to wait for the result?" Miss Taylor said.

Mary shook her head. She would go home and get on with some work unconnected with the Votes-for-Women Campaign. She couldn't do it justice.

"I'll come round and tell you what name they choose as soon as I hear," Miss Taylor said. "I'm sure you'd like to know."

Mary shrugged. She thought she knew already.

When she had finished tea she went upstairs to get on with her homework. Tomorrow was Saturday and she'd go round to help Mrs. Watkins with her shopping. At least that much good had come out of the business. She had made a new and special sort of friend. Mrs. Watkins would understand when she told her she had failed. She would be disappointed but she wouldn't blame Mary.

She went to the window to look out onto the street. Her father was just getting back from work. He looked up and, seeing her at the window, waved cheerily. She waved back. A woman turned into the road and she recognized Miss Taylor.

She was not sure she wanted to know what name the governors had chosen, but she went downstairs to find out.